Dalton Borne is a cowboy who keeps his past closed up inside. He's watched his partners at the New Horizon Ranch find love and he's happy for them and even envious. But his past prevents him from believing he deserves a future that includes a love of his own. But then one stormy night he rescues a very pregnant Rae Anne Tyson from floodwaters and ends up delivering her baby on the side of the road. Suddenly Dalton's life is turned upside down and no matter what he believes he does or doesn't deserve—he can't walk away from helping Rae Anne.

DALTON

New Horizon Ranch, Book Five

DEBRA
CLOPTON

Dalton

This book is a work of fiction. Names and characters are of the author's imagination or are used fictitiously. Any resemblance to an actual person, living or dead, is entirely coincidental.

CHAPTER ONE

Torrential rain poured down relentlessly. Dalton Borne slowed his truck to a crawl and eased along the flooded road. Water swirled across his windshield faster than his wipers could swipe it away and he squinted through the filmy glass, as if that were going to help him see well enough to estimate the creek overflow. It had to be at least a foot deep; he knew the road dipped a few feet ahead and would get even deeper while the water flow grew faster.

Despite knowing better than to cross here when the water was rushing over the roads like this, he continued forward.

The downpour and flash flooding had come on fast and he'd thought he could beat it before the creek got over the banks. He'd been wrong.

Another time, another torrential downpour filled his thoughts, causing the memories of that fateful night to lay heavier on his shoulders. He tightened his grip on the wheel and tensed automatically. He shook his head and tried to regulate his breathing, fighting off memories that couldn't be changed. Memories that, despite three years passing, still hit him hard at times like this. He struggled to focus on what was going on around him now…he needed to turn back. Flash floods in Texas weren't something to ignore.

Pressing the brake, he brought his truck to a halt and reevaluated the situation as the sound of his heartbeat roared in his ears as loudly as the storm outside. Despite wanting to ignore the warning signs, he pulled the gearshift into reverse and began the careful process of backing up. Running off the blacktop was not what he needed to do at this moment. Angling the truck around, he drove back the way he'd come, more than ready to get out of this storm. Needing to get out before the memories drew him too deep. A flash of red off to the left of the road caught his attention.

Dalton straightened in his seat and stared between the swipes of the wipers, trying to get a clearer view through the rain. His heart stalled when he realized what he was seeing.

Taillights.

"No way," he muttered, knowing it was true. That was taillights out there in that darkness. He rammed his gearshift into park. "This is not good."

There was only one place that car could be and that was stuck in a small stand of trees at the edge of the river.

Someone had been swept off the road by the flood.

Miraculously, they'd been stopped by the trees before being swept downstream into deeper water.

He had to get to them. And there was no time to waste.

Stuck where it was, it might last but the danger of it being dislodged and swept away was a problem because the water was rising fast.

He yanked his cell phone out of its holder at his hip, jabbed a few numbers—no signal. The storm had killed what little service there was out here.

He'd been repairing a fence a few miles back on the outer edges of the ranch when the storm hit. The New Horizon Ranch was a big spread and it took him and all four of his other partners to keep it running smoothly. He was more than grateful now that he'd been out here working or whoever was in that car might not have had the chance of being found.

He'd learned that the hard way that second chances and rescues didn't always happen…

Acting as quick as possible, he snapped on his flashers, grabbed the big beamed flashlight from the seat and opened the truck door. He'd brought the truck to a stop in a couple of inches of water and as he stepped into the downpour, his boots sank into water. It didn't quite cover the tops but he knew that even an inch and a half of water could pick up a car or a heavy truck and sweep it off the road. The vehicle caught in the trees had found that out. It had foolishly thought it could get across the foot-deep water swirling fifteen feet down the road from where he was parked.

His hat shielded him a bit from the rain. Still, rivulets of water ran down his face as he lifted the toolbox cover in the truck bed and pulled out a coil of rope and slung it over his shoulder…just in case he needed it.

With no one else to help and not sure what he would find, he tied the rope to the cargo tie-down on the truck bed and then he moved into the water, letting the rope out as he went. The water was moving fast but at this point it was manageable. It was the last ten feet to the car that would be deeper and a faster current. He reached the edge of the drop-off and stepped into the knee-deep water. His boots sank into the mud; he focused on balance and pushed forward. He couldn't see movement in the car. That had him worried. If he had to carry someone from the car to his truck, he prayed the water didn't rise much faster. It was going to be a rough go coming back.

By the time he reached the back of the car, the water was up to the doors and the only reason it wasn't higher was because the vehicle had come to a halt on high ground.

He stepped up onto the bank and moved to the far side of the car. The hood was crammed into the embankment and the trees but there was room for him to get to the driver's side door. His heart stalled when he saw a woman hunched over. He knocked on the window and she turned to look at him through the rain-soaked glass. Even in the blue light of the dashboard inside, he could see how pale she was. And her eyes were as big as the steering wheel.

He lifted the handle and eased the door open. "Ma'am, are you injured?" He leaned forward to be eye level with her and that was when he froze. *Surely not...* He stared from her pale face to her stomach. "Ma'am, are you pregnant?"

"Yes," she gasped, and then grimaced as she grabbed her rounded belly. "And I'm in labor. Have—been—for a while—" She bit the words out through clenched teeth. Before Dalton could completely comprehend the full force of what he'd just waded into, he heard a small *child's* voice from the backseat.

"Are you our angel here to *wes*cue us?"

Dalton forced his head into the car. Water poured from the brim of his hat onto the poor woman, who yelped as he found the little boy sitting in the darkness, strapped into his car seat. He looked to be about two or three. Dalton wasn't a man to feel faint very often but a wave of nausea rushed over him. He had floodwaters rising—already it was starting to seep into the floorboard of the car—and he had a woman in labor and a toddler in the backseat. And on top of that, the wind was billowing as if a tornado was stirring the air.

He sucked in a deep breath and focused. These two—no, three, he amended, thinking of the child who was very nearly here—were counting on him.

And he could not let them down. Failure wasn't an option.

Rae Anne Tyson gritted back the panic that had a grip on her as violent as the labor pain that had just ripped through her. She'd been praying for the last twenty minutes for the Lord to send help. For Him to overlook her bad choices and take control, for her children's sakes.

She had really gotten her and her children into a mess…a life-or-death mess. Something she hadn't foreseen. Yet if there had been a little planning involved in the decision to travel, she would have avoided this.

She could have at least stopped in the larger town thirty-five miles back when she saw the weather was going to get rough. At least then she could have prevented the possibility—the disaster—of giving birth and sinking in floodwaters.

What kind of mother was she to put her babies in this dangerous predicament?

She looked into the concerned green eyes of this cowboy, who was her only hope, and gratefulness overwhelmed her.

"Please. Help Joey. Get him to safety." She would have doubled over in pain if the steering wheel wasn't in her way. Instead, she grabbed it and held on, fighting back her moans and the need to scream as she'd been fighting them down for the last few contractions. She couldn't scare Joey.

"How close are they, ma'am?"

His words, a deep drawl that resonated through the fog of pain in a commanding, reassuring way, had her twisting her head to look at him.

"Five…maybe."

"That's close, right?"

Okay, so maybe not as commanding as she'd thought. She nodded. "Close," she managed, huffing as the pain intensified to unbearable. This didn't quite feel right. They were too hard. Too painful. Was something wrong or did her fear have them intensified?

His eyes widened, but his jaw set in a stubborn jut. "You hang on. I'm getting Joey out of that car seat. Hold on. We've only got a few minutes so we're going to have to get this done in one go."

"No. No way. Get Joey. First." She bit the words out, wanting at least one of her babies safe.

He moved away from her door and she heard the back door open and him speaking to Joey in a calm tone as he told her little one his name was Dalton. She realized her feet were now wet. The water was coming into the car. Dear God—her mouth went dry with the prayer. Her throat constricted and her abdomen spasmed harder. A groan tore from her.

Her cowboy was back in a second, holding Joey in his arms. "Okay, are you in between contractions?"

"Almost. Take him out first, please?" She rested her head on the steering wheel and held on as the pain began to ease.

"I'm not leaving you and that baby behind, ma'am."

She glared at him. "You have to."

"No, ma'am, I don't." His voice and the look in his eyes were steel.

She could tell there was no need to argue with him and she didn't have the energy. If she wanted Joey safe, she had to comply.

"Then we better go before I start having to push," she warned and saw the color drain from the cowboy's face.

"Can you walk?" To his credit, his words were calm.

Rae Anne truly did not know whether she could or not. She nodded. “Help me get out of this car.”

He offered his arm and she grabbed it, digging her fingers into hard, strong muscle. Reassuring muscle. He was going to need a lot of strength, she was afraid.

She grunted as she twisted around and placed her feet into the water. A gasp escaped her at the shock of the cold water swirling about her calves.

“Are you okay?”

She nodded and held onto his arm as she stood. He set Joey on the front seat, pulled a length of rope and tied it around his waist and then tied it around her, just beneath her breasts. He didn’t say anything as he worked, just secured them and then reached for Joey.

“You got a rope on you,” Joey stated.

“Yes I do. Now it’s your turn, little fella.” He took the last of the rope and secured it around Joey before he took him onto his hip and reached for her.

“You ready?”

Her mouth was going dry and she felt a new twinge. Terror filled her. Was she about to go into another contraction? She couldn’t. Not yet. “I’m ready.

We have to hurry."

He nodded and then they started to move. His arm came around her waist after they moved down into the deeper water that was almost to her thighs. The force of the water pushed and pulled and she clung to the first thing her hands found: his belt. Joey talked as they went, blissfully excited about being in the rain and unaware of exactly how much danger they were in. She thanked God once more for that and threw in a few more fervent pleas to get them through the floodwaters to the big truck she could see waiting for them.

She stumbled and went down but his strong, iron grip held. He hoisted her back to her feet and clamped her to his side as he practically carried her forward. Rae Anne felt the clutches of a fresh contraction reaching for her as they started up out of the deep water.

"Contraction," she gritted. A gasp tore from her as a pain so powerful overcame her, she couldn't stop the cry. Her knees buckled and she went down on them.

"Mama!" Joey cried.

The cowboy wasted no time lugging her up with

one arm as he hoisted Joey over his shoulder like a sack of potatoes. He scooped her up into his arms, and then he plunged forward the last few feet to the truck.

One minute, they were outside; the next, he had the rear door opened and had deposited Joey into the seat and then her.

He worked the knot from his rope and slipped it from around his waist. He tossed it to the floor and slammed the door. Rae Anne lay back in the seat.

"Joey," he commanded from the front seat. "Get on the floor and let your mom lay on the seat. Can you do that for me?"

"Yes, sir. I can do it," she heard him say in his sweet, determined little voice. *Her tough little man*, she thought as a contraction hit her full force.

Rae Anne grimaced and started her breathing exercises, fighting to control the pain. There was no way they were going to make it to the hospital.

Joey stared at her with wide eyes. "It's okay, Mama. You can stop making funny faces. We're safe."

She tried to smile. Her precious boy might never forget this night.

She just prayed his baby sister was going to be alright…and would stop being so impatient to come into the world. She needed to hold off for a little longer before making her entrance. But Rae Anne didn't think that was going to happen…her baby was coming.

CHAPTER TWO

Dalton rammed the truck into gear, never so scared in all of his life. He'd delivered his share of calves. But a calf and a baby—not the same thing.

He did not want to deliver a baby!

From the panting sounds coming from the backseat, he feared he was all out of luck.

And the poor woman was in so much pain. She'd been tough out there, fighting through that flood while in labor. She'd been something. And he couldn't let her down. Indecision warred inside him, twisting him up like a pretzel.

"Ma'am, how you doing back there? You're going to have to let me know if I need to stop and help you in any way."

"Keep driving," she growled.

Her command startled him. "Okay, you got it."

The rain blinded him as the wipers worked to move the water off the windshield. He held the steering wheel with both hands. He could not have a wreck with a kid sitting in the floorboard and a pregnant woman having a baby. There was too much at stake for him to mess up and get them in a ditch. He figured they weren't going to make it to the hospital.

Think, Dalton… Norma Sue Jenkins.

Dalton sat up in the truck. The ranch woman and her husband Roy Don lived ten miles down the road. Norma Sue was perfect: capable, and she would know what to do. Plus, she was a woman. And in this situation that was a good thing.

"Ma'am, you hang on ten miles and I can get you to someone who'll know how to help you. Just ten miles. Okay?"

The kid popped up and hooked his elbows on the

seat to look at him. "Is that far, mister? 'Cause my mama, she's nodding but still making them funny noises. Something is bad wrong."

"It's going to be okay, buddy. Your mom is in some pain but that's normal when you have a baby. It's going to be okay. I promise." *What was he saying?* He sent up another prayer—a record for him considering he and the Lord weren't on the best of terms. But he was desperate and he hoped this time his prayers would be heard.

The rain started to let up five miles down the road and he pressed the gas pedal harder. The entrance to Norma Sue's came into view. He took it and then gunned it on the gravel drive. He started honking the horn furiously as he wheeled the truck into the circle drive then slammed to a halt near the door. In seconds, Dalton had hopped from the truck and yanked open the back door. Holy smokes, the woman's eyes were huge as she glared at him.

"Hurry," was all she said as he slipped his arms beneath her legs and back.

"Wait for me, Joey. I'll be back." And then he

stomped through the rain to Norma Sue's back door. Thankfully they'd heard his horn and the door opened.

"What's going on?" Norma Sue hurried out onto the porch, with Roy Don behind her. Alarm flashed over her face as her gaze took in the woman in his arms and she realized he was carrying a pregnant woman. "Is she in labor?"

"Yes, ma'am. You're the closest person I could think of to help her."

"Roy Don, hot water and towels," Norma Sue commanded. A take-charge kind of woman, she wasted no time. "Follow me, son."

The robust woman had on a fuzzy blue housecoat. She hustled into the house and headed down a hall to the first door, where she pushed it open and headed to the bed and yanked off the quilt. "Put her right there and go help Roy Don. Tell him I need lots of towels."

Dalton glanced at the woman. She looked small on the big bed and he found himself hating to leave her. But she was in better hands than his, so he headed out to find Roy Don and then to go get Joey.

This was going to be a night he would never

forget. He just hoped the baby and mother would be safe. He didn't want to think about what would have happened if he hadn't come across them.

Roy Don was in the kitchen, setting a big pot of water on the stove.

"Norma says to bring lots of towels. I've got to get a little boy out of the truck. I'll be right back."

He found the poor kid sitting on the seat, looking scared out of his wits. Dalton smiled at him. "Your mom is going to be okay. Come here and I'll take you inside."

It was then that Dalton saw the big tears and his heart melted. "Come on. It's okay. I promise." The boy came to him then, and wrapped his arms around Dalton's neck. Dalton hugged him hard and carried him through the rain and into the house.

Roy Don was disappearing into the bedroom down the hall with a stack of towels when they got inside. Seconds later, he came out of the bedroom and shut the door behind him. "Well, who do we have here?" He grinned.

"I'm Joey. You got my mama?"

"Your mama is fine. My wife is helping her and she told me to tell you to come to the kitchen and have some ice cream while you wait on her. Does that sound good?"

The boy nodded and relief surged through Dalton. *It was going to be okay.*

They followed Roy Don into the kitchen. He left for a minute and returned with two towels. Dalton wrapped the kid in one and set him in a chair and then he tried to dry himself off a little so he wouldn't keep dripping on their floors.

Roy Don pulled some ice cream from the freezer, dished up a bowl and set it in front of Joey. The boy beamed like a Christmas tree at the sight of the chocolate treat.

He'd just taken his first bite when a baby cry rang through the air.

Rae Anne held her baby girl in her arms and smiled at the woman who had delivered her.

"Thank you. I don't know what we would have

done without you. And the man who saved us from the flood." Her heart still hurt thinking about how close to disaster she and her babies had come.

Norma Sue smiled a wide, engaging smile. "You had an ordeal, that's for sure. But the good Lord brought you through. And getting rescued by Dalton Borne is a bonus—that cowboy is one handsome wrangler."

Oh, he was that. She was tired and worn-out but she wasn't blind. "He did a great job. Could you tell me how my little boy is doing?"

"You hang on and I'll go check."

Exhaustion weighed down on Rae Anne as she watched Norma Sue hustle out the door before she focused her attention back on her precious baby girl. Her dark lashes rested like tiny feathers against her skin. She was all soft and pink and perfectly adorable. Rae Anne blinked back tears of joy and relief. Despite what her ex had put them through, Rae Anne wouldn't have given this darling girl up for anything.

"Mama!" Joey's exuberant exclamation had her smiling as he ran into the room in front of Norma Sue.

"Up you go." Norma Sue lifted him up so he could see his sister.

Joey went still and placed a hand over his mouth and then reached out to touch her. "It's a baby. Where'd she come from?"

Rae Anne laughed—of course he would ask *that*. "I'll explain later. The important thing is she's here and she's your sister. What do you think?"

"She's pink."

Rae Anne and Norma Sue both chuckled.

"Yes, honey, she is. But she'll get less pink soon."

"Will her pointed head go away too?"

Norma Sue covered her smile and Rae Anne studied the slight oval form of Grace's head. "Yes, it will. Babies come like that—"

"Did my head point like that?" His hand went to the top of his head and his eyes widened as if she'd just told him something horrible.

Fighting her smile, Rae Anne nodded. "Yes, but now it's all flat and you are very handsome."

He crossed his arms to study the baby and then looked up. "Mama, Dalt says that one day I can go horse riding with him."

"Oh, he did? Well, we'll see about that."

"He's my favorite." Joey had been on a favorite kick lately so it wasn't a surprise that the man who'd carried him out of a flood would become his favorite. She liked him a lot herself. She didn't want to think about what would have happened to them if he hadn't shown up. Or if her car hadn't gotten stuck on that clump of trees. Her car might have ended up buried in a ditch under water—she shivered thinking about that and her heart raced with the thought.

"Okay, little fella," Norma Sue said in a happy voice. "Time for you to go play with the men in the other room. Mama and your sister need to take a nap."

"I don't need no nap."

"No sir, you are a big boy and have been on a great adventure today, so no nap for you."

"Give me a kiss." Rae Anne felt tired and very thankful, not only for Dalton and their safety but for this woman. Norma Sue had been a godsend. "And meet your baby sister Grace."

He kissed her and then bent forward and kissed

Grace on the forehead. "Sleep good, sister. I see you later, alligator."

Norma Sue led him out into the other room and soon returned. "He's gonna be fine. I think we should call the ambulance, though. You need to go to the hospital so you and baby Grace can be checked out, just for precautions."

She hated the risk of going to a hospital—it might lead a trail here. But there was no way of getting around it. "That sounds good. But what will I do with Joey?"

Norma Sue smiled gently. "Well, I know you don't know me but I could sure keep him for you while you were there. It'd be an honor for him to stay here. I think he's bonding with Roy Don. We could take him over to our boss's house and he could play with their two little ones."

Rae Anne had been in some tough situations in her life but this was one of the hardest. Leaving her son with practically total strangers would have been scary if she hadn't just spent the last hour with this wonderful lady.

"I would be forever grateful to you for doing that for me. He's really no trouble…at least no more than any normal three-year-old boy."

"We'll get along just fine. Don't you fret about that at all. Let me take this little darling while you catch a little shut-eye. You rest while I make the call."

Norma Sue took the baby and Rae Anne's eyes drifted closed instantly…and she found herself reliving the flood and a handsome cowboy appearing out of the storm to save her.

Dalton Borne. She liked his name. She liked him.

She needed to talk to him. But that would have to wait…just a little while.

It had been a long time since she'd had anyone in her life who she could call a hero…and she wanted a chance to talk to him. To thank him.

CHAPTER THREE

"You did what?"

Dalton held the phone away from his ear as Rafe, one of his partners on the ranch, heard his words.

"Yeah, she was having a baby when I pulled her and her little boy out of the car. But everyone is fine so far. They're taking Rae Anne to the hospital soon and I'm going to follow the ambulance. She told me she was moving here and has a place rented but she doesn't know anyone around here. I hate to let her go alone without someone she's at least familiar with being there."

He told Rafe more about what had happened.

"Wow," Rafe said in disbelief. "Anything we can do to help?"

"I really don't know at this point. I'm sure it might help if Sadie, Maddie, and the others came to visit—that might be nice. You know, give her some comfort or something. Norma Sue has been awesome and her and Roy Don are watching little Joey. He's a cute little dude. I'm sure her and her friends are going to have him spoiled rotten by the time his mama gets back."

"You're probably right about that. Dalton, you did good, buddy. I'll tell Sadie and I'm sure her and the girls will know just what to do."

Dalton had had a knot in his chest ever since he'd discovered Rae Anne and Joey in the floodwaters. He felt some relief now. "Thanks. I'm heading there now and since I'll be losing phone service any minute, I'll let you go." As if on cue, he lost the connection before he could hang up.

Through the pouring rain, he concentrated on the taillights of the ambulance. His mind raced with everything that had happened since he'd seen Rae

Anne's taillights in the darkness. The forecast had said that by midnight there was only a twenty percent chance of rain. He hoped so. Tomorrow he planned to go back and see whether her car had survived. If it was still stuck in the trees, then he'd haul it out and see what kind of damage had been done. But tonight he'd make sure mother and baby were taken care of.

He wasn't even sure she'd want him to be at the hospital but since rescuing her, he felt responsible for her. He hadn't felt responsible for anything other than himself in a long time…he liked it that way. He'd worked hard to keep it that way.

But he had to do this.

And for the first time in a very long time, it felt good to be reaching out.

Rae Anne was drained by the time the ambulance reached the hospital and they were both checked out and pronounced healthy. Knowing that her baby was okay took a load off her shoulders. When they took Grace to the nursery, Rae Anne closed her eyes. Tears filled them immediately and seeped from the corners as the reality of the day haunted her.

A light tap on her door had her wiping the dampness from her cheeks as a gentle, very masculine voice asked whether he could come in.

Dalton.

"Come in," she called, and her pulse escalated. And as the handsome cowboy entered the room, her heart fluttered—she was, after all, a woman and after what the man had done for her and her babies…how could she not feel awed by his presence? And oh so very grateful.

She smiled and tears welled in her eyes all over again.

He yanked his hat from his head and held it between both hands as he stood just inside the door. His dark-brown hair was mushed, which was expected after the night he'd also had. His serious gaze held hers. "I just wanted to make sure you were okay. That you got settled in."

She nodded, trying to find her voice through the emotion that clogged her throat. "Yes. Please come closer." She swiped at tears again. "I'm sorry. I'm an emotional mess right now."

"Rightly so after what you've been through." He moved nearer to the bed but stopped a couple of feet away.

She couldn't help herself as she reached out her hand. His forehead crinkled as he looked at her hand. For a moment, he didn't move. And then he enclosed her hand with his.

Heat and electricity converged and sparked through her like lightning hitting an electrical wire. Rae Anne almost gasped but managed not to. If he'd felt it, his expression didn't show it but he gently squeezed her hand. She found her reactions to be inappropriate despite the circumstances. And that made the tears and emotions she was feeling surge more—and there was nothing she could do as wet droplets trailed down her cheeks.

Dalton looked momentarily horrified. "No, don't cry. You're safe now," he offered kindly, as if understanding the feelings warring inside her.

Her voice caught and she pressed her lips tightly

together for a moment as she tried to contain the emotions. He squeezed her hand and she took strength from his support. "I know that I and my children probably owe you our lives. If you hadn't come along—"

His brows dipped. "I did come along and that's all you need to focus on. Don't think about what could have been. It didn't happen. You're okay. Your babies are okay. All is well."

All is well. Rae Anne let that remark fill her. She nodded, trying hard to believe it. How long had it been since all had been well in her life? She couldn't even calculate it. But right now, in this moment, it was.

"Because of you," she said. "Thank you. You were a blessing to me and my babies tonight."

"I'm glad I was there." He squeezed her hand, and she realized he still held it. He smiled but his eyes suddenly looked troubled and he released her hand. "I'm glad y'all are safe." His voice was gravelly and he cleared it. "Can I, um, get you anything? *Do* anything for you?"

Stay. The thought ricocheted through her. She shook her head. "No, I'm fine. I just need to rest. It was a hard day." She wished for the gentle reassuring pressure of his hand holding hers again. "You've done enough. I'm sure you need to head home for the night."

"Yeah, sure. But if you need me." He pulled a card from his pocket and handed it to her. "That has my cell number on it. If you need anything, anything at all, you call. I'll be here. I'll check on Joey in the morning but I can tell you he's in good hands with Norma Sue and Roy Don. They're good people and highly regarded in ten counties around here."

She smiled at that. "Thank you. They were lifesavers for me too. As were you."

"Oh, believe me, they saved my life too. I'm not sure what I'd have done if I'd had to hunker down and deliver the baby. You definitely got blessed by Norma Sue being home to help." He looked almost sheepish when his lips turned up in a half smile.

Rae Anne laughed from shock at her reaction to him—thankfully he thought it was from what he said. *Goodness, Dalton Borne could stop traffic with that smile.*

And hearts.

"Sleep well, Rae Anne," he said, his voice a touch husky. And then he headed to the door. He paused there to look back at her. "You call if you need me."

And then he was gone. Heart stuttering, she looked down at the card.

New Horizon Ranch was embossed across the center of the card. At the bottom, it said Owners: Rafe Masterson, Maddie Rose, Chase Hartley, Ty Calder, and Dalton Borne. Each person's number was beside the name.

Dalton was an owner of one of the largest ranches in the area.

Even she'd heard of the ranch. Mule Hollow, Texas had a huge ranching community, Mr. Overton had told her. She studied the card for a long time, and then curled her hand around it and fell into an exhausted sleep, safe in the knowledge that tonight she didn't feel alone.

Tomorrow she'd stand on her own two feet again. As she had been doing forever, it seemed. But tonight…she took comfort in knowing he, Dalton Borne, was just a phone call away.

CHAPTER FOUR

Dalton sank into the waiting room chair and leaned forward to rest his elbows on his knees as he stared at the floor and tried to let the emotions grappling inside him calm. His hands shook and he clasped them together. He figured the Lord had looked out for Rae Anne today by putting him in her path.

Today he'd been at the right place at the right time.

Memories of another time threatened to overwhelm him, though. A time when he'd been at the wrong place at the wrong time. A time when the people at the hospital hadn't welcomed him in. Hadn't thanked him…instead, they'd cursed the fact that he'd been where he'd been—he pushed the thoughts away.

Not forgetting them, though. He'd never forget them, but he'd learned to keep them at bay, not letting them past the barriers he'd constructed around them. Barriers he'd had to build in order to move forward into some semblance of living. Tragedy was hard to get past. Hard to let go of. And despite knowing that he hadn't been in the wrong in the accident, that hadn't changed the fact that people had died…a child had died.

And he'd walked away.

Dalton breathed slowly and sat up in the chair. He forced himself to stand, to make his legs carry him forward. Just like he'd managed to force himself to go on living after the accident.

Minding his own business and working with the land and cattle had been his saving grace. There was a peace that came with the work he did. A peace he could sink into and focus on. In this place, he could control his life to some extent. Focus and not think too far out. Not think about the things in his life that that split second in time had changed for him…and for them…Amanda and little Martin. Dalton's palms dampened and his heart raced; the room spun. He was used to this, deserved it. He took deep breaths and let them out slowly as he focused on the only thing that helped. It didn't absolve him, didn't redeem him in his own mind but it helped him function…it hadn't been his fault and he'd done everything he could do.

Other than not being on that road at that time, there had been nothing he could do to prevent that wreck itself.

Still, that stormy day three years ago, a mother and child had died and he'd been helpless to save them. Today—today he'd saved a mother and two children.

He focused on that…but it didn't take the pain away for two who'd died.

"Sir."

Dalton was standing by the window; he turned to find a young nurse looking at him with concern.

"We're going to take good care of them. The baby

is in the nursery now, sleeping peacefully. If you want to see her, you can."

He nodded. "Thank you."

"Just around that corner. And, sir, visiting hours are over, and on this wing we try to enforce that where non-family members are concerned. I'm sorry, but after you see the baby you'll have to leave."

He needed to go anyway. He could go wait downstairs in the emergency room waiting room but what good would it do? Rae Anne and the baby were in good hands. And he wasn't family.

He stopped before he made it to the nursery. The baby was fine. And beautiful as he looked through the window and watched her sleep. There was nothing more for him to do.

Turning away, he headed toward the exit.

Rae Anne was just finishing feeding Grace when the nurse poked her head in the door.

"You have visitors if you're up to it."

Visitors? Who? Rae Anne didn't know anyone

from around here other than Dalton and Norma Sue and Roy Don. That was it. Maybe they'd come to check on her.

"Sure." She sat up a little more.

"I'll let them know."

Rae Anne had just enough time to wonder again who they were when the door opened and four women about her age walked in. One was dark headed and dressed in jeans, boots, and a bright-blue cotton shirt that brought out the color of her eyes. She strode rather than walked, and there was a confidence about her…as if she could take on anything. It was obvious she was a cowgirl. The other one, tall and willowy, had long cinnamon-colored hair and wore a soft mint-green dress with sparkly sandals. And the third woman was small; her hair was a deep auburn with golden highlights sparkling in the morning sunlight from the hospital window. She wore white jeans with a gauzy top. The last woman into the room also wore blue jeans tucked into fancy boots with red tops.

"Hey there," the dark-headed cowgirl said. "I'm Maddie Rose Masterson. I'm one of Dalton's partners and he told us about what you went through last night. We wanted to come by and introduce ourselves and see if there was anything we could do for you and your little family."

"I'm Sadie Masterson," the willowy one offered. "I'm married to Rafe, one of the partners, who just happens to be Maddie's husband's twin. We'll give you a test later to see if you can remember all of our names." She smiled and tucked a strand of her long cinnamon-colored hair behind her ear.

Rae Anne chuckled. "Okay."

The short one with the beautiful deep auburn hair smiled. "And I'm Amber, also married to a partner."

"And I'm Mia. Soon to be married to a partner. We're so thankful Dalton showed up when he did. That area is dangerous—they've warned me about it and now I know it's true."

Rae Anne's heart was about to pound out of her ribcage as everyone introduced themselves. *Dalton had sent them.* That was about the sweetest thing anyone had ever done for her—other than save her from a raging flood. That would never be topped. How could she ever repay him for that? A lump formed in her throat and she looked down at her sleeping baby girl.

Oh dear God. She was almost overwhelmed every time she thought about what could have happened. Between overactive hormones of a new mother and the traumatic events leading up to the birth, she was a mess.

She blinked hard and focused on the women Dalton had sent. "It's so nice of all of you to come. I don't know what to say. But, please excuse me if I tear up. I'm a little emotional."

Maddie grinned. "We are a bit overwhelmin'. And don't you worry—if you feel the need to bawl, you go on and do it. We understand."

"True," Amber said. "We do understand. We were wondering if you were just passing through or were you coming here to live?"

"Or to visit someone?" Maddie interjected.

"We, ah…" Sadie broke in, "want to make sure you have a place to go when you and the baby leave the hospital."

"That's right." Mia smiled at her. "We want to

offer you a place at the ranch if you don't have a place to stay."

"But..." Rae Anne was shocked speechless as she stared at the four smiling women. "No, I mean, I couldn't—but thank you. How awfully nice. Really." *Truly*. "I have a place rented. The address is in my purse. I was on the road where the house is when I ran into the water."

"You were?" Maddie asked. "Where would that be? I'm trying to think of any vacant properties..."

Rae Anne's stomach twisted as she reminded herself that she had nothing to fear from these four women. "I don't remember the address. I'll have to try to get it out of my car, if it's not sunk downriver somewhere. But, they call it the old Overton place, I think."

Everyone looked back at her with blank looks on their faces and then Maddie's eyes sparked. "Wait, I think that's what I remember someone calling that deserted place across the road from the ranch."

Sadie cocked her head slightly as her expression turned to puzzlement. "But, Maddie, there's nothing on that place but a—"

"Who rented this place to you?" Maddie cut Sadie off.

"I…er, knew the owner. Mr. Overton. He rented it to me." He hadn't exactly rented the house to her but rather told her to use it for as long as she needed to because he would never need it again. She wasn't one who normally took handouts from people but she was desperate and old Mr. Overton knew this. She'd not told the sweet old man anything about her personal nightmare but he'd known something wasn't right in her life. He'd picked up on a lot of stuff without her having to tell him. People in the nursing home weren't always the sharpest of minds but Mr. Overton had his moments of pure, sharp clarity. She'd refused at first to admit anything or to accept his offer.

But she'd finally been desperate enough to accept it. She even had a note he'd given her to use as an agreement if anyone should ask.

Now, seeing the expression on Maddie and Sadie's faces, unease filled her. "Is something wrong?" She rocked Grace gently—as much to soothe her own nerves as to comfort the sweet angel in her arms.

"It's a little rough." Maddie looked as if she hated to tell her this news.

"Oh, I'm sure I can clean it up in no time."

Maddie and Sadie glanced at each other. And then Maddie smiled sweetly. "I hate to break it to you but, Rae Anne, the house across the street from the ranch might not be livable. Our ranch has been leasing the land for a while and we run cattle over there. It's a long-term lease made by CC, our former boss, and the owner of that property. But, the house hasn't been lived in for years."

Rae Anne's heart sank as she looked at her visitors. *Had she come all this way for nothing?* She fought for positive. "I'm sure it will be fine. Nothing a little soap and water can't clean up. Mr. Overton assured me the last time he checked it, that it was in great shape."

Mia stepped up. "I haven't seen the place, but what if we go over there after we leave here and we check it out for you?"

"Check what out?" Dalton came into the room.

Rae Anne's stomach clenched at the sight of the rugged cowboy in the doorway. He was as good-looking as she'd remembered from the day before. She hadn't imagined it and it was something she was determined to ignore.

"My rental," she said, not liking the way her gaze was drawn to his. Yes, she owed him for saving her and her babies but that did not in any way, shape, or form mean she owed him anything other than gratitude. She was not interested in a man. Not a good, bad, or amazing one.

"She's renting the Overton place."

"The *Overton* place?" Dalton looked momentarily confused as he looked at Maddie.

Rae Anne didn't miss that something passed between the two and that look caused a new unease inside her. Something *was* wrong.

Dalton gave her a somewhat reassuring look. "We'll be neighbors. The nurse says you're about to be released. I was able to get your car towed to the ranch this morning. And I stopped by the store on the way in and a clerk helped me buy a car seat for a baby, since I noticed you didn't have one inside your car."

"You bought me a car seat?" Shock at his thoughtfulness rocked through her. *Who was this man?*

Maddie grinned. "Dalton, that was quick thinking." Maddie looked at her. "If you haven't already figured it out, Dalton here thinks fast on his feet, which comes in handy on a ranch."

"The nurse told me before I left last night that in order to get Grace home she'd have to have a seat. So I got you one. Now, if you want me to, I can give you a ride. Or if you'd rather ride with the ladies, I'm sure they'd give you a ride too."

Rae Anne felt more overwhelmed by the whole situation. She wanted to tell him no thanks, that she'd get her own ride but he'd been so very helpful. And in truth, she couldn't allow herself to believe all men were jerks just because she seemed to have the worst luck where they were concerned.

"Thank you. I'll ride with you. You've gone to so much trouble that I hate to burden you more but I'm in no position to stand on my own at the moment."

The women started to talk at once.

"That will work out perfectly. We'll go on now, ahead of y'all, and gather up a few things and meet you at your place."

"Yes," Sadie agreed. "Don't worry about anything—we'll have the house ready in no time for you and your babies."

"I'm excited," Amber added. "I know you probably hoped to get settled in before Grace was born but sometimes life throws a curve and when it does, it's always good to have friends to count on."

Maddie touched her arm. "And that's where we come in. You don't need to worry about anything. We've got this. Oh, and I almost forgot." She held out a duffel bag. "I packed a few loose-fitting clothes in here. Dalton said your suitcase was in the car so I got to thinking you might need clothes."

"I do. That was so thoughtful."

Maddie winked. "Glad we could help. And there's always room at the ranch it *huge,* so don't worry, you'll have a roof over your heads one way or another. Got it?"

That overwhelmed feeling crushed down on Rae

Anne again. She had grown so used to fending for herself this last year that this was all nearly too much to take in. "I don't know what to say."

"Nothing. Now, take care of her, Dalton." Maddie winked at her and then they all headed out of the room and left her and Dalton alone.

But before either of them could say anything, the doctor came into the room. He smiled at Dalton and held out his hand. "Congratulations on a beautiful baby girl."

Rae Anne bit back a gasp. Shock registered on Dalton's face and then he quickly masked that shock with a smile.

"I agree she's beautiful. But I'm not the father. I'm…a friend. A neighbor. I'm here to give them a ride to their home."

"Oh, sorry." Not missing a beat, the doctor smiled at Rae Anne. "Looks like you have good neighbors."

"Yes, the best," she said. And it was true.

After the doctor left, the nurse came in and helped her while Dalton went to get the truck. When she and Grace were ready, the nurse rolled them downstairs in a wheelchair to the entrance where Dalton waited beside his truck. He had the back door opened and she could see the baby carrier. Her throat tightened; the scalding heat of tears burned the back of her eyes and throat.

What would she have done without this man?

CHAPTER FIVE

Dalton had been shocked when Maddie had said Rae Anne was renting the Overton place. The house sat off the road, surrounded by pastures that would have gone to ruin like the house if they weren't leasing it for their cattle to graze on. Part of the long-term lease was that they also kept the fences up and the barns—but the house wasn't included in the lease that CC and the owner had written up all those years ago. He'd often looked at that house and felt a shadow of sadness for the waste of it. He wondered whether the owner was ever going to reclaim the land. The ranch had a long-standing first option in place for if the owner ever wanted to sell. So far, nothing had been accepted. And now, to learn that Rae Anne and her children were supposed to move into it, really threw him a curve ball.

It really wasn't his place to just come out and tell her that there was no way in…the world that he could let them do it. It was what he wanted to say, though, and he kept reminding himself on the hour-long drive from the hospital in Ranger back toward Mule Hollow that this wasn't his responsibility. Rae Anne might not appreciate him butting into her business any more than he already had.

They talked about the storm and about her car and he told her a little about the ranch as they drove through the country. He told her that her car was in pretty good shape, all things considered, and that it shouldn't take too much work to get it dried out.

"That would be unbelievably wonderful," she said. "I'm really going to need my car."

He liked her voice, the soft huskiness of it. "I'll start on it tomorrow."

"I honestly do not know what I would have done without you. And now you're going to work on my car. I'll have to repay you somehow."

He glanced from the road to her. "There's no need for that."

Stubborn light came into her eyes, like he'd seen yesterday when she'd gotten out of that car while in labor and had started toward high land. "I will find some way to repay you. Even if it's dinner, if nothing else."

Focusing back on the road, he tried not to think about how she made him feel. Dinner with her sounded…perfect. But not gonna happen.

Silence fell between them for the next several miles. "You'll want to stop in and see the Overton place. You should see it first, before you show it to Joey. You know, assess the place up close."

"So, is it really that bad?"

"Truth is I haven't been any closer than fifty yards to the place in the time I've been at the ranch. I've tended to the cattle and the fences but haven't ever driven across the cattle guard into the actual fenced-off yard."

"Then I'll take your suggestion. Joey's been through enough without me adding any more stress to his little life. Not that at three he'll even realize the situation isn't perfect. Knowing him, he'd think it was an adventure to move into a disaster."

Dalton grinned at that and shot her a glance. "I can see him doing that." A few more miles down the road, the entrance to the New Horizon Ranch came into view. He still had moments that he couldn't believe CC had left part of the ranch to him.

"Wow, that's a beautiful place." She studied the impressive stone and steel entrance. "That says New Horizon Ranch. This is the ranch you're part owner of?" Green pastures dotted with huge oak trees and dark cattle stretched out before them. The house could be seen just over the rise.

"That's it. CC Calvert didn't believe in building anything that wasn't a showplace. And this was his showplace."

"You can say that again. I'm speechless and I'm seeing it from a distance."

He hated to tell her, but speechless was coming in a few moments when she saw her house. He slowed and turned down the plain gravel road that signaled the entrance to the Overton place.

"The Overton house is just over the hill. Rae Anne, I think you need to be prepared for disappointment. Like we said, it's been vacant for years."

"It'll work out." She focused on the view in front of them. He drove over the hill and there it sat: a tan house with shutters that were falling off and knee-deep grass. They did send their man over with the tractor every once in a while to keep the grass cut down because the cattle couldn't get over the cattle guard to graze it.

"Oh goodness," she gasped. Her mouth fell open in shock.

Despite reminding himself again that this was none of his business, he couldn't help himself. "Let's not get too ahead of ourselves. It does look bad. But, I've never been inside. Maybe it's better than it looks."

She clamped her mouth shut and then nodded like

a jackhammer. “Right. Right,” she repeated and glanced at him with determination in her eyes. “As long as there are no holes in the roof or the floor, then anything can be fixed. I mean, if you really look at it, and think cut grass and fixed shutters, it’s cute.”

He wasn’t so sure he was seeing what she was seeing but he wasn’t about to disagree. Not when he had a feeling she was hanging on by her fingernails.

What looked like uncertainty filled her eyes and Dalton got the feeling that she had no idea exactly how scared she looked in that moment. “We’ll get it figured out,” he offered.

What was her story?

The question went round in his thoughts like a revolving door.

Why was she here, thinking she could move into this dump? As if wondering the same thing, her gaze shifted from him to the sleeping newborn in the backseat. She stared at her child for a long moment; she set her jaw and she stared from him to the house.

“You were right. I’m glad we came before we picked up Joey. I need to go inside and see what it looks like." She took a deep breath…her shoulders slumped. And she dropped her forehead to her hand. "I may have really messed up."

He gripped the steering wheel hard to keep from reaching out and laying an encouraging hand on her shoulder.

She looked at him before he could say anything. "You probably think I'm some kind of total mess-up. And believe me, I am beginning to think the same thing. But I have two little kids who are counting on me so I have to salvage this."

"And you will." This time, he did touch her—a gentle squeeze of her thin shoulder. "Come on. Let's go look."

"I may have to go to a hotel for a few days—until I'm able to get around a little better."

She'd just had a baby. There was no way she was going to get this house ready, even if it was move-in ready. She needed help.

"Let's go inside, do a quick assessment so we know what it looks like. Then we'll go pick up Joey and I'm taking you to the ranch tonight. There is plenty of room, so don't even think about going to a hotel. No use even thinking about arguing because Mule Hollow doesn't have a hotel."

"But—"

"No buts—have pity on me. The gals would have my hide if I didn't take care of you tonight." It was all true. "Maddie already told you there was room."

"You have already taken care of me far more than anyone should expect of you. But okay," she said, with an I-give-up hint of a laugh. "I wouldn't want you to lose your hide."

That urge to touch her hit him again like a sucker punch from a hard left hook.

Rae Anne wasn't in a position to say anything except thank-you. She reached for the door handle, suddenly needing to get out of the confines of the truck. The way she was drawn to everything about Dalton Borne was getting out of hand.

He bolted out of the truck the moment she made a move and hurried around to grab her elbow before she'd set a foot to the ground. Gently he held her by the arm as she eased to a standing position. Movement was still a bit uncomfortable but as she looked up at him, the memory of her being in his arms rushed back.

What was wrong with her?

The last place she wanted to be was in a man's arms. Hadn't she learned anything from her last two experiences?

Yes! That she was no good at picking men.

And that was a lesson she didn't plan to ever forget.

"Are you okay?" he asked, and she thought he looked as stunned as she felt.

She nodded quickly. "Fine. Could you help me get the baby out of the car?"

"Sure. Should I just leave her in the carrier?"

"Yes. If you don't mind carrying her in it. I'm not quite able to carry that yet."

"I've got it." He opened the door to the backseat and after a moment, emerged carrying the sleeping infant in her baby carrier. "She's snuggled down nice and happy in this thing."

Rae Anne laughed. “She’s so cute.”

With a baby and carrier in one hand, he placed his other hand at her elbow as she walked to the house. The tall grass was a little creepy and would need to be mowed immediately. She hoped there was a lawn mower stored somewhere. She squinted up at the beautiful blue sky with the white, gently drifting clouds—such a different day than yesterday. The sweet scent of honeysuckle was heavy on the breeze and she glanced around to see the large overgrown bush on the edge of the house.

“Do you have a key?” Dalton’s question broke into her thoughts.

“No. But Mr. Overton said it would be behind a door plaque.”

A wooden plaque hung beside the door with an *O* on it. She reached her hand behind it and found a key hanging from a tiny nail. Relief swamped her. Mr. Overton hadn’t been wrong about the key. Though he’d had a fuzzy memory when it came to the condition of the place, the key being there was a plus.

Dalton took the key from her and opened the door.

Pushing it wide, the stale scent of pent-up air welcomed them—it was not sweet and fresh like outside had been.

She peered into the dim room. It was furnished but everything was covered in a layer of dust. "Let me go first," Dalton said, but she'd already stepped forward—straight into a cobweb.

She fought it off, panic grabbing her as she frantically swiped at it.

"Here, let me." He took over pulling the creepy web from her borrowed blouse and gently swiped the clinging web from her hair. He looked down at her with concern. "Nothing to worry about. I'm sure we'll find several of those as we move forward. I'll go first."

Her breath had escaped her as she looked up at him. All she could do was nod. *She had to get a grip. Really.* "Thank you. I'm more than a little embarrassed that I'm feeling so helpless. It's really aggravating."

"May I remind you what you've been through in the last twenty-four hours? You're tired but certainly not helpless."

It was actually the last forty-eight hours that had

been hard but he wouldn't know that her fast departure and spur-of-the-moment decision to come here had also taken its toll. "Well, I'm feeling that way. But I'm going with your excuse for me because that means there's hope that tomorrow I could wake up and be Supermom."

His mouth hitched into a smile that caused her toes to tingle.

"I'd say you already are. You survived a flood while in labor and then gave birth all in one night. Yup, Supermom is in the house."

She chuckled. "Okay, so if you put it that way, it does sound pretty impressive."

"Yeah, that'd be an affirmative." He led the way across the living room and around the corner into what was the kitchen.

"Oh," she said. "It's not as bad as I feared."

"Yeah." He set the baby carrier on the counter and looked around. "I'm truly shocked that it's not any worse than it is."

The cabinets needed painting and cleaning but the countertop was granite and the floor was hardwood. "It has great bones to work with."

Car doors slammed and a moment later, chatter filled the air as Maddie, Sadie, Amber, and Mia clomped up the steps and entered the living room. Rae Anne's heart swelled with gratitude as she saw the bags and realized they were full of an array of cleaning supplies. Mia brought up the rear and was carrying several brooms and mops. It was obvious these women had come to work.

"Hey, don't start crying. This is just what neighbors do. And believe me, more are on the way. I called Norma Sue and she's making a few calls to her posse. They'll be here directly and she'll be bringing Joey. Y'all can go to the ranch house while we take care of this."

Not cry? How could she not cry at this kindness? Tears swelled in her eyes and slipped down her cheeks. "I don't know what to say. I've made such a mess of this for my babies and I'm so ashamed. Thank you all."

Dalton slipped his arm around her shoulders and the comfort of him there completely undid her. She sniffed and then just started to cry. The next thing she knew, he'd pulled her into his arms so that she could bury her face against his chest.

“There, there,” he soothed. “You’ll be alright.”

“I don’t know what’s wrong with me. I’m not usually this emotional but this is a big deal.”

“It’s your hormones.” Sadie came up to pat her on the back. “You’re doing a good job helping out, Dalton,” she added and Rae Anne did not miss the hint of amazement in her tone. Rae Anne wondered about that…what about Dalton being so helpful called for such shock?

“I’m just glad I found her last night.”

“We are too,” the women all said behind her. Rae Anne was grateful, too, and realized she felt safe once more in the circle of Dalton’s arms.

And it was a really nice feeling.

However, she knew all too well that feeling safe was an illusion that she couldn’t afford. The minute she let her guard down, she could be letting down her little family.

She had no time for tears, hormones or not; her children needed her to be strong and to get off the pity party. She dried her eyes and stepped out of his arms.

“Thanks,” she managed and then turned to the

four women who were gathered around. "Y'all are amazing."

"Just call us the cleaning crew." Maddie grinned. "We'll get the place cleaned up and our men will get the outside looking spiffy and make sure the plumbing is working right since it's sat empty for so long."

Amber studied her. "You are going to the ranch to rest."

"But..."

"Nope, no buts allowed. You're going now."

Rae Anne couldn't put up much of an argument. Exhaustion and soreness had taken its toll.

Within minutes, she was in the truck with Dalton and her baby. They drove across the street and up the drive toward a huge, gorgeous sandstone home with a large porch and gigantic windows. Yes, she could see instantly that Maddie hadn't exaggerated. There was definitely room for her and her children here for the night if they needed somewhere to stay.

Dalton used the cordless drill to drive a screw through one of the crooked shutters and into the wood of the house to secure it once again. It had been two hours since he'd settled Rae Anne and her children at the ranch. Things were shaping up. This was the last shutter to hang and Cliff, Maddie's husband, was helping him and that had made things go much faster than if he'd been hanging them by himself. The two of them had tackled the shutters while Ty and Rafe were inside checking out the plumbing and Chase was helping the women move heavy stuff around inside as they cleaned the old house from floor to ceiling.

"I have to say this place is in decent shape, it seems." Cliff finished the last shutter. "I had my doubts when you called and told me what was going on."

"Me too. It appears to be more cosmetic fixes than structural and that's fantastic. I have a feeling Rae Anne needs a little good luck in her life."

"Sounds like it." His expression shifted to dismay. "I can't imagine Maddie being in a flood and in labor. It makes me sick to think about it."

"Yeah. Don't I know it…when I opened that car door and realized what was happening, it's the most scared that I've ever been in my life."

"I hate to say it but I'm glad it was you and not me."

Dalton was glad it was him too.

The women's laughter from inside drifted outside through the open doors. Norma Sue and her friends Esther Mae Wilcox and Adela Ledbetter Green had arrived right after he and Rae Anne had reached the big house. Adela had stayed over there to keep Rae Anne company and help with Joey and the baby while her two buddies had come to help clean. He had a feeling it had been a carefully decided upon plan as Adela was about the sweetest, most adored female in these parts. If Rae Anne had anything she needed to get off her chest or needed to confide that she needed help in any way other than some house cleaning, then he figured Miss Adela would be the one she'd confide it to.

He had a gut feeling that Rae Anne was hiding something and might just need a friend she could talk to.

CHAPTER SIX

Rae Anne had fallen asleep in a plush bed in a downstairs bedroom fit for a queen. It was gigantic, with wide windows that offered a view of the back pastures and the cattle that dotted the landscape. Dalton had explained to her that this had been the master suite and after CC Calvert left the ranch to him and his other four partners that they'd all moved out of the bunkhouses into the house; Maddie had taken this room and the guys had all moved into rooms upstairs. The room was vacant now and she was welcome to use it for as long as she needed to.

As he'd been telling her that, a large pickup truck pulled up and Norma Sue had hopped out, along with a redhead whose name was Esther Mae and a soft-spoken petite woman with kind eyes and white hair that framed her face and showed off her amazing blue eyes—Adela.

Adela had taken care of her while everyone else left to go work at her house. If she hadn't been so exhausted, she might have protested but she was long past that. Joey had seemed to have taken up with Adela and gratefully Rae Anne had handed over Grace for a little while so she could get some rest.

Now, she woke feeling a little like road kill. Having already been through childbirth with Joey, she knew the reward of her sweet babies far outweighed a little pain. Still, she would be glad when she didn't hurt anymore and she had no plans for more children. She loved them desperately, despite their no-good daddies. She was grateful to have them, but she had no plans to ever let a man get close to her again. She'd sealed her heart up and that barrier was there for good.

So why, she wanted to know, had her mind gone

straight to thoughts of the handsome cowboy rescuer as she sat up in bed?

Because it was logical, considering she owed him so very much for rescuing her and her babies. She'd never stop thinking about the man. And now he and his friends were over there cleaning up her house so she and her babies would have a place to live.

She pushed the thoughts away and eased out of bed and headed to the bathroom. When she was finished, she washed her hands and splashed cool water on her face in hopes of bringing a little color to her cheeks. She found a brush and used it to smooth some of the tangles out of her hair. For now that was the best she could do.

She opened the door and walked down the short hallway, pausing at the entrance to the great room. It was empty so she continued on to the kitchen, where she smelled a wonderful scent of soup cooking.

Adela greeted her with a smile.

"Oh, don't you look rested. Come and sit down. The baby is sleeping right here." An oblong clothes basket sat on the table and it had a blanket folded in the bottom for a cushion. There was Grace, sleeping soundly. "Sometimes you just have to make do with what you've got."

"This is perfect. Where's Joey?"

"Dalton came over to check on you, and Joey wanted to go with him so, I hope you don't mind, but he went over to 'help' get his mommy and baby sister's house ready. And Dalton will take good care of him, as will everyone there."

Rae Anne smiled inside and out. "He's a sweetie. I'm sure he's fine." She would evaluate the situation later but today there was nothing to do but let him spend time with Dalton and the others.

She sat down. "Everyone is so wonderful to help."

Adela had crossed to the stove and was filling a bowl from the large pot on the stove. She set the steaming vegetable soup in front of her. "God put you right where you are supposed to be and placed the right person in your path to help you. I hope you like vegetable soup. I felt like it would nourish you and also be a good comfort food."

Rae Anne inhaled the savory scent. "The scent

alone makes me all warm and fuzzy inside."

The older woman chuckled. "Good. Now how about some sweet tea?"

"It sounds heavenly." She was lifting her second spoonful of soup when Adela brought two glasses over and placed one on the table for her and the other in front of Rae Anne.

"How do you feel?" Adela sat in the chair across from her.

"Much better. I should be moving around a lot better tomorrow." She took a drink of the tea and then another. The zap of sweetness would give her a little more energy for the moment until the soup kicked in. She hadn't really eaten much since the ordeal in the car and she knew that now, with a baby and an active three-year-old, she was going to have to eat to be able to keep up with her little family.

"So, where are you moving here from? If you don't mind my asking?"

"I'm here from the Pearland area." Adela looked as if she was too polite to ask more when Rae Anne knew she had to be very curious—as were all of the people working on her rental right now—as to why a pregnant woman as far along as she was would decide moving at this late date was a good idea. It was a terrible idea but all she had had at the moment. She offered up her excuse: "I waited a little late to make the move and Grace is a couple of weeks early, according to my due date. That's why I got myself into this terrible mess."

Sweet blue eyes twinkled as Adela patted her arm. "I'm just glad you're safe."

Grace stirred and Adela rose to gently lift the baby from the makeshift crib. "I believe a sweet angel is hungry."

Rae Anne held her arms out and took her daughter. After thanking Adela again for the food, she moved back into the bedroom to feed her. Thanks to some rest and the hot soup, she was beginning to feel stronger. And that was a very good thing.

"Watch me!"

Dalton looked up from where he was nailing a

new board onto the front porch railing. He'd learned quickly that Joey needed eyes on him at all times. The three-year-old thought he was a mountain climber or something. And to prove it, he was now on the outer edge of the porch, hanging onto the railing while maneuvering his feet between the porch spindles. It wasn't dangerous, really, considering the porch was only about a foot off the ground but the kid thought he was Superman. In his little three-year-old mind, he probably thought he was scaling Mount Everest and wasn't the least bit aware of danger. If Dalton wasn't careful, the kid might be on the roof before the day was done.

Leaving his hammer on the steps, Dalton strode to where the boy was hanging on and grinning up at him. His bright eyes dug deep into Dalton. "Come on down from there." He reached for Joey.

"No!" the kid declared and grabbed hold tightly. "I climbing."

Dalton couldn't help laughing.

"Looks like you've got your hands full," Cliff called from the end of the house where he was working.

Dalton shot him a don't-I-know-it look and then focused on the boy again. "How about you come help me hammer a nail instead of climbing?"

Instantly, he had Joey's attention. "I can hammer."

Dalton chuckled. "I bet you can."

"Dalton," Norma Sue called from inside the house. "Can you come in here for a minute?"

"Sure." He looked down at the little guy in his arms. "Let's go see what the ladies are doing first and then we'll hammer."

"Makin' a house fer my mama and baby sister. They told me."

He laughed. At three, it was obvious that Joey knew everything. His mom was in for it when he got older. Dalton had been keeping up with what the ladies were doing off and on all afternoon but he hadn't been inside in the last hour. Cliff followed them in, and Ty and Rafe were in the kitchen as they entered. They'd been working on the back porch.

Esther Mae Wilcox stood beside the kitchen counter with a big smile on her face. Her red hair had cobwebs in it but she didn't seem to care. The house was a hub of action as females came in from various areas to join him and Joey in the kitchen.

"We've got the place cleaned up pretty good," Esther Mae said. "I even jumped around in a few spots to make sure the floor wasn't going to fall in."

Norma Sue harrumphed. "Felt like an earthquake when all that jumping was going on."

"Very funny." Esther Mae scowled. "Anyway, it seems solid. But we thought you could run over there and see if Rae Anne feels like coming over to tour the house."

Norma Sue's brows knit above concerned eyes that darted to Joey and then met Dalton's. "We're not real sure she should be over here all by herself in this, um, catastrophe." She said the last word quietly as if Joey understood the word in the first place.

Joey looked up at him. "Dalt, what ca-tras-toti mean?"

He rubbed the kid's dark hair. "It's nothing. Let's go get your mom. Want to?"

The boy squealed at that. "Yes!"

Amber laughed from across the room where she was perched on the arm of an old couch that he sure hoped they weren't planning to leave in the room. "You've got your orders, cowboy."

He headed out of the house a few minutes later, leaving everyone else to continue their work. Once in his truck, he surveyed the house again and was impressed by the results of friends pitching in with concentrated effort. The windows that had been smudged with years of grime now gleamed from the gallons of glass cleaner that Maddie and Sadie had applied. The porch looked better and the straightened up shutters helped substantially.

All things considered, from what the house had looked like to what it looked like after a herd of determined people had attacked it, there was no comparison.

But was it livable for a newborn?

He hadn't known Rae Anne long—though it seriously felt like longer than two days—but he still couldn't picture her here in this house.

For some reason he didn't quite understand, he

could picture her in *his* house. And that thought blindsided him. He had no plans to ever have a woman in his house—in that way.

He was still telling himself that when he pulled up to the big house that was getting emptier and emptier as all of his partners had married off and moved into smaller homes either on the ranch or near the ranch. The sight of Rae Anne sitting on a porch swing was unexpected. Something in his chest tightened when she looked up and met his gaze across the yard. She was rocking Grace and the picture was so…perfect that it took his breath away.

Stole it right out of his lungs like the kick to the chest from a two thousand-pound bull.

And despite the fact that he had the air conditioning inside the truck cranked up on high, he felt as though it was suddenly a hundred and fifty degrees inside the cab.

"Mama, Mama, Mama," Joey chanted from the backseat, reminding Dalton that he wasn't alone.

Holding onto his senses by a thread, he tore his gaze away from Rae Anne and looked over his shoulder at Joey. “You sit tight while I go see if your mom wants to go see the house.”

“She do.”

Dalton left his door open and headed to the patio. Rae Anne had risen and her head was tilted slightly as she watched him approach.

“Is everything alright?”

“Yes. Why do you ask?”

“You look…upset. Is Joey okay?”

He stopped short, realizing his tumultuous thoughts must have translated into his movement and his expression. “No. I mean yes. He’s fine. He’s in the truck. I just had…” He lost his words. She was gorgeous. She still had the dark circles under her eyes but she wasn’t as pale as she had been, and her eyes were brighter. She seemed more centered. “I came to see if you would like to come see the house. The crowd of ladies over there are wanting to see what you think. But only if you feel like it.”

Adela came out of the house, carrying two glasses of water. “If you feel up to it, I’ll watch the baby.” She set the glasses on the table.

"That would be wonderful. Thank you. They've worked so hard. I need to thank them and admire their work. I can't wait."

She handed over the baby and walked slowly toward the truck. Dalton fell into step beside her and then helped her inside and they were on their way. His insides churned as she turned slightly in the seat and talked to Joey. The kid jabbered about climbing the porch and helping out.

"I helped Noma Sue."

"I bet you did. Do you like our new home?"

Dalton saw the little tyke nod vigorously in the rearview mirror.

"Good. It's going to be wonderful. You're going to have the country to run and play in and we're going to make you a swing."

"And I go fish'n'!" he said gleefully. "Fish'n's fun."

Dalton laughed at the declaration. He shot Rae Anne a glance and she was laughing, too, with joy in her eyes.

"Yes, you'll go fishing too."

Dalton wasn't sure why they were here in this rundown home but he felt the powerful urge to make certain that they were happy here. He thought of the family that was always at the back of his mind. The one that would never get to enjoy the simple act of fishing or swinging with their child. That sick feeling gripped him; his hands tightened on the steering wheel and he sucked in fresh air. Holding his breath, he let the moment pass and then slowly, silently let the pain take him and then he let it go. As best as he could. There were some things that could never be changed. He knew over and over that he'd been told he wasn't responsible for the accident that left mother and son dead but that didn't mean he didn't take responsibility for it. Always would question everything about the moment when their lives collided and he came out alive and they hadn't.

For all of his life, it would haunt him. His heart had begun to race and he focused on turning the truck onto the blacktop and traveling the few feet it took to get to the drive on the other side of the road that would lead to Rae Anne's new home. This little family had been thrown into his life, too, just like the Bolts, but this family would have good times to share with each other. And he was forever grateful that he'd had a part in ensuring that was possible.

Rae Anne's gasp brought him out of the past. "It looks so much better already. The shutters—they aren't falling off anymore."

"Funny how a small thing can make a big impact sometimes."

"Tell me about it. Did you do that?"

"Me and Cliff, Maddie's husband."

"I'll have to thank him. He's also your partner...*Rafe's* twin brother?" she asked, hesitating on Rafe's name as if she'd been hunting to remember it.

"That's right."

"Sorry to repeat information but I have a lot of people to thank and I'm not sure I've made all the connections with names and faces. So I might ask several times until I get them figured out."

"I don't mind. And it's understandable." He pulled to a halt and cut the engine. "Everyone has pitched in."

"Me too," Joey piped up from the back.

"Yes you did." Dalton climbed out and went around to Rae Anne's side. She had gotten out and was reaching for the back door.

"I'll get him. The last thing you need to do is try to lift him out of that car seat."

"Right. It's a habit. Thank you for getting him."

In a few minutes, he had the little dude out of the seat. The boy wrapped his arms around his neck and held on, so Dalton carried him up the steps and pushed the door open for Rae Anne.

She stopped just inside the doorway. Her hand pressed against her heart as she let her gaze drift around the room. Her expression was one of awe.

The place still needed work but he had to admit that it looked good. A lot better than it had.

"Oh my goodness," she murmured.

"What do you think?" Maddie came around the corner from the kitchen as everyone came from different directions in the house.

"I—" Rae Anne started to say but her voice broke.

"What's wrong, Mama?"

Dalton had the overwhelming urge to put his arms

around Rae Anne as tears glistened in her beautiful eyes. He forced his boots to remain planted two feet away from her.

"It's just so wonderful," she managed. She scanned the room. "Thank you. Each one of you. I don't know what I would have done without all of you stepping in to save the day."

Pride swelled in Dalton's chest as he looked at his friends. They'd stepped up to the plate and welcomed a young mother in need with open arms. But more than that, they'd backed it up with deeds. This place might need a ton of work to get it completely turned around, but at least it was clean and livable now. A ping of regret hit him about that.

Had he hoped that maybe they'd be stuck at the ranch house longer?

Yup.

The answer that echoed through him startled the daylights out of him. He had no place in his life for wishes like that. None at all.

CHAPTER SEVEN

Rae Anne sat in the chair and rocked her baby as the most wonderful people she'd ever met swarmed around her, making dinner for her and her children and making beds—after they'd scrubbed the house down and made it shine. The sun had gone down and darkness had settled in around her new home like a cozy blanket. For now, at least she felt safe.

Mr. Overton had told her that this place was a good place for her and her little family to heal and he was right. He had been the most intuitive man she'd ever met.

"Okay." Esther Mae hustled out of the kitchen. With her red hair and her canary-yellow warm-up suit, she was walking sunshine. "We've got you fixed up with food for the next few days. You might not want us popping in and disrupting your life every few hours but the least we could do was give you food to eat."

"We've even tucked a few in the freezer for you, too," Norma Sue added. "Are you sure you don't need one of us to spend the night and help you out, honey? Any one of us would love to stay."

"I'll be okay. I…I really want to have the time with both babies. I'll call Maddie if I need someone."

Maddie came out of the back room holding Joey's hand. "We finished making the beds. And Joey here helped me get that little folding crib set up in there for now, until your furniture arrives. That baby will need a real mattress soon."

Rae Anne would have to take care of that as soon as she could but for now she was grateful for the portable crib.

"I helped." Joey climbed into the rocker with her. He placed his hand on Grace's head. "You got a bed, little sister."

How had she been so very lucky to have ended up here? "Thank you all. I think we'll be settling into the beds pretty soon and be just fine."

Adela had come out of the kitchen and now stood beside Esther Mae. "So we're going to go now and let you have some time to yourself."

"But," Maddie added. "You call if you need us. Dalton is only two minutes away if you need some muscle. And the others aren't too far away."

"I'll be fine and I promise I'll call if I need anything."

Everyone started to talk at the same time. None of them looked convinced that she would be okay alone. It was touching that they were so concerned but she was certain that she could handle everything on her own now. Still, everyone assured her that they were available if she needed them.

"But remember." Esther Mae shot a pointed glance at Dalton. "Dalton is the closest to you, so if there is an emergency he is the logical one to call."

"That's right," Norma Sue agreed heartily. "He

could get here faster than Applegate Thornton can spit a sunflower seed—and that's fast. So call him. Isn't that right, Dalton?"

Dalton had been standing beside her, listening but not saying much. Now he got a strange look on his face as he looked at the two older ladies. It was almost a wary expression. "Rae Anne knows I'll be here if she needs me."

"That's wonderful," Esther Mae gushed. "I'll sleep better tonight knowing you're on call."

Rae Anne didn't know what was going on but there were some heavy currents passing through her living room.

Maddie chuckled as she looked at Dalton. "So, now that we have that all settled, I think we should all head out and let this little family get some rest."

More chuckles and twinkling eyed glances were shot at Dalton, who seemed to be scowling more with each look. A few more minutes and finally everyone was in their vehicles and taillights were disappearing down the road.

And finally, Rae Anne and her family were alone. She was forever grateful to everyone but she'd needed this. Needed some time alone with her babies. Dalton and the curious currents that had been in the room earlier had her distracted, though. *What had been going on?*

"I like them, Mama." Joey looked up at her. "They made me cookies."

She hugged him close. "That's because you're such a good boy. And you're going to be the best big brother in the whole world. What do you think about your sister?"

He peered into his sister's sleeping face. "Her sleeps a *lot*. But I like her. Can she play with me?"

"Well, babies do sleep a lot and she's not big enough to play with you yet. But soon."

Joey yawned. "Okay." He leaned his head against Rae Anne.

It was time to get him tucked in.

"Let's get you ready for bed and I'll tell you a bedtime story, okay?"

"About a horse?"

"Yes, about a beautiful black horse. Now, hop up and let's go. While Grace's sleeping." Joey raced down the hallway to the first bedroom, where she'd told them to set the beds up. She wanted to be as close to the kitchen as possible. And the old house wasn't small, though it wasn't huge either. But she would want to be as close to the kids as she could at all times.

She placed Grace into her crib and then decided not to worry about baths until morning. It had been a long day.

Rae Anne had left everything behind except her photos. Everything in the room had been donated and everyone had assumed the moving van with all her belongings would be arriving soon. But nothing was coming. And that was okay, because she had what was important. She had her babies and they were safe. Dalton had brought all her suitcases inside. She was lucky because the water level had stopped at the car's bumper and had never actually gotten inside her car other than the floorboards when they'd opened the door to get out of the car. If she hadn't gotten stuck on that incline, she would probably have lost everything inside the car. Again, more to be thankful for.

She snuggled in beside Joey, hugging him close in the crook of her arm and feeling more blessed than she could fathom.

"Story, Mama." He yawned.

She kissed his forehead and then began the story…making up a story about a horse and a little boy and a great adventure in a new place.

She'd barely started and he fell sound asleep. He ran at ninety miles an hour but when his gas ran out, Joey fell asleep quickly. Kissing his forehead, she eased out of the bed, tucked the covers in around him and slipped out of the room.

She knew she needed to take advantage of the moments both babies were asleep but she couldn't do that at the moment. Instead, she walked through the house, trying not to think about all the work that still needed to be done. Despite knowing this, she saw the possibilities.

She didn't know how long they would be here in the house, though. Mr. Overton had told her to make it her own and to stay as long as she needed to but she really didn't know that much about him. For all she knew, there could be family the house belonged to now. She was here temporarily and as soon as possible, she'd find a place they could actually settle in.

She was in the living room when she heard Grace whimper and then she began to wail.

Hurrying into the room, she scooped her baby out of the crib, grabbed a diaper and headed out of the room. Joey, miraculously, continued to sleep.

Taking Grace to the couch, she sat down and talked gently to her baby as she changed her wet diaper. When that was done, she settled into the rocking chair to feed her.

Contentment settled over her as she looked down at her baby girl and a renewed determination filled Rae Anne—she would make a life for her children and she would not fall prey to a man ever again. Yes, there were good men out there and she knew that; Dalton Borne was one of them. But this wasn't about her really bad track record of picking the liars with something to hide in their past. No, that wasn't ever going to happen again because she was going to stand on her own two feet from here on out.

She would raise her children here in this wonderful community. She'd increase her assistant job and was thankful she had a job she could do from her home and online—she'd just need to get Internet set up soon. With the clients she had now, they'd live on a tight budget but they'd make it.

Other women did it every day and so could she.

And with any luck, when Grace's daddy was released from prison tomorrow, he wouldn't come looking for her.

With any luck, the no-good, sorry excuse of a man would have no care that he'd fathered a daughter. And he'd have no idea that he went to prison because Rae Anne had given the cops the info they needed to catch him.

CHAPTER EIGHT

Two weeks had passed since Rae Anne and her little family had moved in across the road. Dalton had stayed away as much as possible but he'd had to check on them a few times. It was the right thing to do. Other than that, he'd let the ladies help her out. And they were all happy to do so. He hadn't missed the way Esther Mae and Norma Sue had looked that first night when they'd settled her into the house. Those two plus Adela weren't called the Matchmakin' Posse for nothing. He'd seen that glint in their eyes when they'd suggested Rae Anne call him first.

He hadn't really known what to do about that then. The posse had never had their sights set on him before but he had a pretty good feeling that his time was up.

They had figured out that Rae Anne didn't have a truck full of furniture coming and had called him immediately to head over to Dottie and Brady Cannon's to pick up a real crib they wanted to lend Rae Anne from the women's shelter that they ran on their ranch. He didn't care about the matchmaking right now; he was just glad to see the concern for Rae Anne and glad to have the crib and mattress for the baby in the back of the truck.

Dalton contemplated digging into Rae Anne's business today. He'd been trying to stay out of her way. Trying to keep her out of his head but she was there. And every day, he wondered more and more why she'd shown up here on the verge of giving birth with only the few belongings she had in her car. He felt from the beginning that something wasn't right about this whole scenario. And when he'd been out at the shelter, he'd run into Dottie's husband, Brady, who was also the sheriff of Mule Hollow. Brady had asked about Rae

Anne, about exactly what was bugging Dalton—was she in some kind of trouble? A pregnant woman with nothing to her name moving to town…it just seemed like a red flag that something wasn't right. He'd told Brady that he'd wondered the same thing but hadn't probed; they'd agreed to keep a watch and that he should see what he could find out. So he had more on his mind than the fact the posse had been the instigators in getting him to be the one to deliver the crib.

Truth was, he wanted to be the delivery boy. He wanted to see her.

She was digging in the flower bed while Joey played with a small tractor in the grass nearby. He spotted the small folding crib on the front porch.

Dalton's spirits lifted just seeing her.

"Dalt!" Joey yelled and raced toward him as he got out of the truck.

"Hey, buddy. How's it going?"

Joey put both his fists on his hips and tilted his head back to look up at Dalton. "I got a tractor."

Dalton chuckled. "That is great. All men need a

tractor."

"Come see." He grabbed Dalton's hand and dragged him toward the yellow tractor.

"Hi," he called to Rae Anne as her son pulled him past her.

"Hello." She smiled and Dalton almost tripped. "Careful. He's a little forceful sometimes."

"I can see that." Dalton was lost in that smile, and the twinkle in her eyes. He'd thought about her for days and realized he'd missed her. Joey tugged hard to try to get him to crouch down, which forced Dalton to put his attention on the boy and his tractor and not Rae Anne. Joey snuggled up close to him.

"See. It digs holes. Mama says no holes but it does it anyway."

Dalton could see Rae Anne biting her lip and his gaze snagged on those lips for a second longer than he had a right to. He yanked his gaze back to Joey. "The tractor digs the holes all by itself?"

The boy nodded solemnly. "Mmm-huh. It does."

"No fibbing, Joey," Rae Anne called softly and Dalton heard the smile in her admonishment.

Dalton bit back a smile this time and his gaze met the laughter-filled eyes of Rae Anne. She stood and dusted her knees off and then her hands. She was getting around a lot better these days. And she looked great. She had curves; he wondered whether they were normal for her or due to just having a baby. Was she normally really thin or was she normally curvy? The fact that he was curious about that made staying disconnected hard. But he was curious. He liked her curves but then, he figured he'd like Rae Anne, any size or shape. And that troubled him even more than anything…because that meant he'd crossed some kind of invisible line. This attraction he felt toward her was getting more and more personal every day.

It didn't matter he'd tried his hardest to stay away over the last two weeks and let others step in and help her out. Nope, distance hadn't dampened his desire to see her in the least.

If anything, absence had made him more attracted to her. He suddenly found himself wanting to tell her what he'd never told anyone: about his past, the pain of feeling responsible for the deaths of a mother and child. The guilt that he'd lived and they hadn't.

The knowledge that he had a life to live and they no longer did…but why would he tell her? Not for pity, or for sympathy. It was what it was and he had no idea how to cope with it other than as he was. Day by day…in silence.

The best thing he could do for Rae Anne and her family was help them out when he was needed but not let himself get attached. Staying away from them would be preferable but impossible.

"I brought you a crib." He was thankful that he'd blurted that statement out instead of what he was thinking…that she was about the prettiest woman he'd ever seen.

"Really?" She glanced toward his truck.

"Yeah. Brady is the sheriff in town and he and his wife Dottie run a women's shelter on their property. They had extras and Dottie heard through the ladies about you and wanted to send it over."

Her smile faltered. "Oh, I'll have to thank them. Did you say he's the sheriff?"

"Yeah, Mule Hollow is really lucky to have the

law enforcement we have. There's not a lot that goes on here but he and his deputies could handle anything that came their way." He found himself watching her closely on that bit of information—considering he'd thrown it out there, acting on his hunch that Rae Anne was in trouble.

She nodded. "That's always a reassuring thing."

"I think so." He lowered his tailgate so she could see the brown crib that lay in pieces in the bed of the truck and the small mattress underneath it. "I'll have to move it inside and put it up in the room. Will that be alright to do now?"

"Yes. Any time that's good for you."

She seemed distracted and that made him all the more curious. *Had he hit on something?*

"Can I help?" Joey tugged on Dalton's jeans leg.

"Sure you can." Dalton pulled a bag of bolts from the bed. "Carry this inside for me."

"Sure," Joey quipped and took the bag.

"Lead the way, buddy." Dalton picked up the headboard piece of the crib. Rae Anne took the lead and hurrying to the porch, she reached down into the portable crib, picked up Grace and tucked her in the crook of one arm and then opened the front door. She stepped back while Joey tromped inside.

"Just put it in the front room. I want her in the same room with me."

"Sounds good." He walked past her and followed Joey into the first room down the hallway. The bed was made and though the crib would take up more room than the portable crib had, there was going to be plenty of room for it. He made several trips out to his truck for the rest of the pieces of the crib and then brought in the tools he would need. Joey trailed him every step. At three, the kid had a determination about him that could mean Rae Anne was going to have her hands full as he grew. But then, just because Dalton had pushed his parents' limits didn't mean this cute little kid was going to do the same to Rae Anne.

"So you want to help me?" He crouched down and surveyed the different parts of the crib.

"Yes."

"Yes, sir," Rae Anne said from the doorway.

"Yes, sir," Joey repeated in that little voice of his.

Dalton smiled. “Good job, big guy. Minding your mama is good.”

“I know.”

At the boy’s quick response, Dalton found his gaze swinging up to Rae Anne’s laughing gaze. She shook her head and mouthed the words, “I’m in trouble.”

Dalton laughed. “We’ve got this if you need to do something else.” The suggestion was as much for himself as for her benefit. With her in the room, he was having a hard time keeping his gaze off her and his thoughts on anything other than her.

“I’ll start supper. And thank you.”

With a mixture of relief and regret, he watched her go and then turned his attention back to Joey and the crib.

Later, they surveyed their handiwork. The crib was set up and all it needed was sheets and it would be ready for the baby. Joey yawned. The little boy had been a good helper, determined to help until they were almost done. Then he’d crawled up onto the regular bed in the room and lay on his stomach and propped his chin in his hands and watched Dalton finish. Now his eyes were heavy and sleep was about to claim him.

Sure enough, in the next instant, Joey's head tipped and he was out.

Moving quietly, Dalton gathered up his tools and eased out of the room. He found Rae Anne working in the kitchen. She'd moved the small crib into the living room and he saw the baby was sleeping too.

He stood beside the breakfast bar at the edge of the kitchen. "I'm done and the little cowboy is passed out in there."

She looked up from where she was mixing up what looked like cornbread. "That's how he is—goes and goes and then finally just passes out."

He knew he should leave but his boots weren't moving.

"Would you like some coffee or tea? Or water? That's all I have to offer at the moment."

He saw the clear coffee carafe was half full. "I'd love a cup of coffee."

She poured the mixture she'd been mixing up into a pan. "Coming right up." She opened the oven and placed the pan inside and then pulled a cup from the cupboard. He noticed there weren't but a few dishes inside the cabinet.

"Do you want cream?"

"Black."

She poured coffee into the mug she'd gotten for him and also the one sitting beside the sink. He moved into the kitchen and his pulse was freaking out like a metal detector that had found gold. She turned unexpectedly and he was too close. The hot cup of coffee hit him square in the chest.

"Oh," she gasped as her expression turned to one of horror.

He gasped himself as the wet heat seared through his shirt. He immediately grabbed the cloth and held it out from his skin to prevent much of the heat remaining to touch him.

"I'm so sorry—" Rae Anne dropped the cup in the sink and grabbed a towel from the counter. "Is it scalding you?"

"I'm fine," he said, as she placed the dishtowel on his chest and frantically tried to soak up the liquid. Her hands shook as she worked.

"Hey, it's okay." He closed his hands over hers. They were standing close; she looked up at him with fathomless blue eyes and he was feeling no pain. "The heat's gone. I pulled the cloth from my skin."

Her hands stilled beneath his and her mouth trembled. "Are you sure?"

Oh, he was sure. Her hands were soft in his and she smelled faintly of sweet flowers. He started to dip his head; kissing her was suddenly about as essential as the air he breathed. But he caught himself almost the instant the thought hit him and he straightened. "I'm fine. How about we try for that cup of coffee again and I won't come up behind you and startle you this time?"

Her brows crinkled. "Are you sure?"

"Positive." He let go of her hands and took a step back—hoping she couldn't hear the thundering of his heart.

"But your shirt—"

"Will dry."

She picked the cup back up, rinsed it off and then dried it and refilled it with coffee. Carefully, she set it on the counter. “There you go. It’s safer that way.”

He chuckled and picked up the cup.

She led the way back out onto the front porch, where there was one chair and an old porch swing. She took the swing and he took the chair. Though he wanted more than anything to sit in the swing beside her.

“How’s your car running?” He and Treb, one of the men who worked for the ranch and was good with engines, had gone over the car and fixed a few issues. Surprisingly, the water hadn’t done too much damage. Dalton was still scratching his head on that one.

“It’s good, thanks to you.” She sipped her coffee and he did the same.

So many questions swirled in his head. He’d thought of her constantly and though he’d stayed away as much as possible, he knew that he probably wasn’t going to be able to keep that up. She had been turning down offers of help now that she was getting around better and he wondered how much sleep she was getting. She seemed okay right now but there were a few shadows under her eyes. *How tired was she?*

And more questions: *Did she have any money? Was she hiding from someone?*

That question alone had kept him up at night. He'd noticed a few things when he'd cleaned out her car and put things out to dry. There was only the bare necessities in that car: clothes, a box of pictures that thankfully hadn't gotten wet, and a few other items.

"So, what's your story, Rae Anne?" he asked after taking a drink of his steaming coffee. It was time to press for answers.

She ran a finger around the lip of her cup and didn't say anything for a few minutes. "What makes you think there's a story?"

"I'm not blind and neither is anyone else in town. There's no moving van bringing your things, is there?"

She held his gaze and then, as if deciding it was time, she shook her head. "No. There is no moving van coming."

Dalton thought he saw trust in her eyes and something told him that she didn't trust easily.

"Are you in trouble?"

Indecision warred in her expression. "Not at the

moment," she said at last.

He'd known something was wrong. Dalton stood and set his coffee on the small table beside the chair. He moved to lean against the porch railing. "Care to elaborate? I'd like to help."

She moistened her lips and his gaze shifted there again. Thinking about what kissing Rae Anne would feel like was completely inappropriate at this moment—he yanked his gaze up and found her watching him. *What was wrong with him?*

"I needed a change." She looked worried.

"I want to know why a woman who was expecting a baby at any moment loaded up her little boy and whatever her car could carry and headed out to a new town. One she'd never been to and a house she knew very little about. What made you make a decision like that?"

She stood and walked off the porch. Her shoulders were stiff as she moved away from him.

Dalton followed her, worry driving him. "Tell me, Rae Anne. What's going on? Were you being abused by your husband? Stalked? What are you running from? Tell me and I'll help you."

"You've done enough. I came here to stand on my own two feet and I will."

Did she think he could walk away and ignore that she was in trouble? He stepped up closer. "Did someone hurt you, Rae Anne?" A ball of anger burned in the pit of his stomach and he found himself wanting to break in half any man who would hurt her.

She swiped fingertips across her forehead. "No. Not like that. Not by lifting a hand to me."

Relief washed through him like the aftermath of a dissipating tornado. "Then how?"

"Look, I need to check on the babies." She started around him but he grabbed her arm and held firm.

"Rae Anne. You came here to hide. I know it and the only way I can make sure you and the kids are safe is to know what to expect."

She gaped at him, and then jerked her arm. "You can't protect me from this. No one can. I need to check on my children."

Too stunned by her refusal and her answer, he let go of her and watched her walk away.

"Wait," he said at last, stalking after her. "That doesn't make sense. You're telling me that something is putting your kids in danger and you won't confide in me so that I might be able to help you?"

She stopped on the porch. "I've already taken up too much of your time. You are not my keeper. You did not make a mess of your life and do not deserve to have to deal with the mess I've made of mine. Besides, I think I'm fine here. I really do. So, just let me be your neighbor and stop feeling responsible for me because you rescued me from that flood."

"I'm not—"

"Yes, you are and you know it. You did your amazing and wonderful deed and I appreciate it. But you don't owe me anything else."

She hurried into the house and closed the door behind her.

"You have got to be kidding me," he muttered. He didn't understand her train of thought at all. Spinning on his boot heels, he stalked to his truck and yanked open the door. Slamming himself into the seat, he hung a wrist over the steering wheel and stared at her house.

Great. Sure. It was none of his business…that's what she'd basically told him.

Got it.

He cranked the engine, revved the motor and then backed around and headed out the way he'd come.

Message received loud and clear.

CHAPTER NINE

Rae Anne was shaking when she closed the door. She'd upset him and she knew it. The man had been offering her help and she'd turned him down. Despite the fact that she needed all the help she could get.

He deserved better from her. But…when he'd taken her arm and looked into her eyes, her pulse had skyrocketed and her knees had gone weak. And then she'd caught him staring at her lips as if he were thinking about or wanting to kiss her.

Butterflies fluttered and swooped inside her as she

remembered.

She groaned. She could not afford to have that kind of reaction to him. To any man. She had made such bad choices in her life. And despite believing with her whole heart that Dalton Borne was nothing like the other men she'd let into her life, she could not let herself fall into a relationship again. She had two babies and bless poor Joey's heart, he'd already had to live through two mistakes. She couldn't put him through another one.

But…goodness, she'd never been as drawn to a man as she was to Dalton.

Still, she had two babies and her future would forever be devoted to them from here on forward.

She heard Dalton's engine roar to life. She moved to the window where she could watch him leave as he pressed the gas and, in a cloud of dust, headed away from her.

Her heart raced. He had helped her. He didn't deserve to be treated so badly when all he'd been trying to do was help her.

Did he deserve to know what was going on in her

life? Did he deserve to know how foolish she'd been?

She closed her eyes and then hung her head. It still was so embarrassing that she could have fallen for the lies…

Grace started crying as she woke from her nap. Rae Anne jerked her head up, feeling as if somehow she'd been caught letting her guard down.

Hurrying over to her, Rae Anne scooped her baby from the portable crib and she hugged her close.

"It's going to be okay, little one. It is. Don't you worry," she said softly as she paced slowly around the dreary room. Rae Anne knew she was speaking to herself.

Now if she could just believe the words.

Dalton watched the calf run from the herd and with the flick of his wrist, he sent the rope flying. It sailed through the air, and looped over the calf's head. Dalton's horse planted his feet and backed up while he wrapped his end of the rope on the saddle horn. The grandstands full of people erupted with applause and shouts of excitement as he catapulted from the saddle, raced to the calf and in a few swift movements had the calf on its side with three legs tied. He lifted his hands in the air, signaling the time's final count and then he stood. More cheers erupted from the stands and he realized he'd won the event.

He raised his hat in salute to the crowd of Mule Hollow residents and many who had come from surrounding counties for the rodeo. Dalton enjoyed the competition, knowing they did this many days on the ranch when they were roping calves to brand or doctor on. In that setting, he didn't have to be the quickest time, but it sure helped his day when he was accurate with his rope. He'd hauled his horse all over the country, racking up points and chasing the lure of the National Finals Rodeo in Vegas every year but not any longer. His competition days ended one cold, rain-drenched instant three years ago. He'd only recently started to participate in these local gatherings at Clint Matlock's indoor arena.

He led his horse out of the gate that one of the other cowboys held open. Bob clamped him on the back and congratulated him. As did the other cowboys waiting to take their chances on the bronc riding that was coming up next. Ty would be competing in that event and Dalton wanted to get his horse put up so he could get back to the stands to watch his friend.

"Man, you were on fire out there." Ty came from the fence where he'd been watching Dalton compete. He fell into step with him as he headed out to the trailer to put his horse up. He grinned. "Kinda looked like you had something to prove."

"Naw," he muttered, sliding Ty a glare. "Just had some pent-up frustrations that came out in the form of concentrated effort."

Ty chuckled at that. "Yeah, like I said—you had something to prove…like maybe you don't have some pretty woman on your mind."

Dalton frowned as he wrapped the reins around the trailer rail and secured them. "Don't you have a horse to ride?"

His good friend's grin only grew. "In a bit. There's a whole herd of us crazy bronc riders waiting to bust our buns out there. You should go up to those stands and say hello to her. She's here, you know."

Dalton hadn't known. Since she'd made it clear she didn't want his help or his opinion, he'd stayed away. Especially when he'd realized he probably couldn't be around her without expressing that opinion. He'd needed to maintain some space to try to put away his feelings for her. Involuntarily, his gaze swung toward the crowded stands.

"She wouldn't welcome me. I'll stay right down here."

"So Mia was right. She told me her and the girls thought y'all had had a fight or something. Said they went to see her and took her grocery shopping with them in Ranger and she seemed a little touchy when your name was mentioned."

That didn't surprise Dalton. After he'd thrown gravel on his exit the other day, she was probably pretty angry with his childish behavior. "Yeah, well, let's just say we're having a difference of opinion. She's not wanting my help these days, so I'm glad Mia and the other gals are stepping in. Something about her past isn't exactly right. I think she's on the run from someone or something. Because she did come clean with me about no moving van of belongings coming like we all assumed. What she had in that car is what she has. Nothing more."

Ty took that information in. His gray eyes turned serious. "Do you think she's in danger?"

"I don't know but I have a bad feeling. When I pressed her about it, she clammed up. I hope we don't have a situation like Chase had with Amber."

Sadie had had a stalker she'd been on the run from, but this didn't have that same feeling to Dalton. *No one can help me,* Rae Anne had said. And then there had been the disgusted comment about her mistakes.

"She doesn't want my help, doesn't want me to feel responsible for her just because I pulled her out of that flood. But…" His words trailed off as he heard them call out Ty's name. "Look, get out there and ride. I'm going to go around to the grandstands area to watch you take the glory." He grinned and Ty laughed.

They were both aware that Pace Gentry was under the same roof with them, as were several ex-rodeo bronc riders. There was some stiff local competition in this event. Not to mention Treb Carson. Before he'd joined the armed services, he'd made a name for himself on the circuit riding broncs until he'd walked away suddenly and joined up. Now getting back to his roots on the ranch, everyone knew he'd hold his own out there in the competition.

"I'll give my all. I enjoy the challenge. You seem to be pretty taken with Rae Anne. Don't let the challenge defeat you. If you think there's something there between you, then you need to grab hold and not be bucked off just because she's pushing you away. There could be something deeper going on."

Dalton stared at Ty. He was a quiet man who didn't waste a lot of talk in long sentences. "I hear you, buddy. Now go. Ride. Don't get bucked off."

"You either." Ty laughed and then turned to head toward the chute.

Rae Anne had jumped up with the crowd and clapped hard when Dalton had won the tie-down, as Maddie had called what he'd been doing.

"Dalt done good!" Joey yelled. He'd been riveted to the event as Dalton and his horse had charged out of the chute. All he'd talked about for the last two days was Dalton. It had been "Dalt this" and "Dalt that." Rae Anne had had to fight telling him to stop talking about his obvious hero.

Her son had every right to idolize Dalton. The man *had* been their hero, after all, and deserved all the admiration Joey was giving him. Honestly, she hadn't been able to get him off her mind. She watched him now as he strode from the back area of the arena and halted at the edge of the steps. Instead of coming up into the stands, he moved to the fence and watched Mia's soon-to-be husband, Ty, lower himself down into a chute onto a horse—that didn't look all that excited about the thought of being ridden. It reared but Ty simply lifted himself up with the hands that he had still gripping the steel bars around the chute. The cowboy standing on the catwalk grabbed the back of his protective jacket—obviously ready to help yank Ty out of there if the bronc got crazy. The horse settled down a little, not enough to suit Rae Anne but enough that Ty lowered himself back down onto its back. He secured himself and then, holding his head down and one arm crooked in the air, Ty gave the gatekeeper a nod. The gate swung wide and the hors—no, the bronc—busted out of the arena in a sidestep that led straight into a leap through the air!

Rae Anne gasped; Joey whooped along with everyone around her. Ty was moving with the wild acting bronc as it kicked and spun and leaped. Ty held on despite all the horse's efforts to toss him. The buzzer sounded and the two cowboys on horses that stood at the outer edges of the action moved forward. One went for the horse's flank and something there he was reaching for as the animal continued to buck. The other horseman moved his horse toward Ty, who slid from the bronc to the back of the other man's horse. They moved out of range of the bucking bronc as the other horseman succeeded in grabbing the strap he was reaching for. Instantly the bronc calmed. Joey went wild, chattering, and she knew her son was forever caught up in the excitement that was a rodeo.

Everyone was congratulating Mia, who sat, transfixed, watching her man.

Maddie nudged Rae Anne and nodded toward Joey. “You might have a future cowboy on your hands.”

“It looks that way. I’ve never seen him so excited.”

“Well, you need to bring him to the ranch and let the guys put him on a horse. He’s old enough to start getting the feel for a horse.”

Rae Anne’s gaze shifted to where Dalton was moving away from the fence and it looked as if he was heading out of the arena area. *Was he leaving?*

“I might. Hey, Maddie, would you mind watching Joey for a few minutes?”

Maddie smiled. “Sure. Go on.”

She didn’t hesitate. Adela was watching Grace for her at the house and so it was the first night she’d been out without her baby; she didn’t have to worry about her. Now she felt compelled to talk to Dalton.

To ease the tension she'd put between them.

He hadn't deserved the cold shoulder she'd given him the other day and it was weighing heavy on her.

"Dalton," she called, catching up to him just as he reached the outside parking lot. He spun and jerked to a halt. Dear goodness, the man looked good in a pair of chaps and a black hat that dipped over his forehead, giving him a sexiness that was undeniable no matter how hard she tried to deny it. And she'd tried ever so hard since the moment she'd first met him—well, after she'd gotten out of the grip of baby pain, that is. When a woman is in the middle of a contraction, even a devastatingly handsome cowboy wasn't getting the nod at that moment.

"Hey," he said, his voice husky and surprisingly gentle.

After the way she'd turned and walked away from him the other day, pretty much closing the door in his face, she expected a less than welcoming greeting.

"That was a great…the roping." She stumbled

over what exactly to call catching the calf. Her expression must have shown her confusion because his lips hitched into a hint of a smile.

"Thanks." He looped a thumb through a belt loop and waited for her to say more as he studied her.

She had, after all, been the last one to walk away and now was approaching him. She should be the one to speak; only, now words clogged her throat. "I…we…" *Breathe, Rae Anne*. "I'm sorry, Dalton. Can we talk? I need to explain."

He glanced around, as if deciding whether that was a good idea or not. When his gaze came back to her, he wasn't smiling. "You don't owe me any explanation." His lips flattened into a straight line as his brow crinkled over skeptical eyes. "You never did. I stepped out of line thinking it was my place to hammer you about your private business. It wasn't."

She moved a few steps closer to him. "Look, I don't trust real well these days and keep a distance between me and…people. It's nothing against you. It's just a fact. And I especially don't want to get close to a"—she paused—"a man."

His jaw flexed and his eyes were shuttered, distant. "It's okay. I get it. I'd like to ask why but I know that's none of my business. I'm just interested in making sure whoever has you running scared and stove-up like this isn't coming around to cause you trouble. Maybe that's not my business, and I understand. But I'm a man and I wouldn't be able to hold my head up if I didn't at least ask to help a woman who I thought needed help."

He was pulling back from any personal attraction to her and her problems. She was now just a woman in need. She should have expected that. It was what she wanted—wasn't it?

"About that." She wanted to reach out and touch him. Caress the jaw that he held so rigid, watch the eyes soften that were so distant from her right now. Eyes that had been full of something far more personal two days ago. "I've made some really embarrassing mistakes in my life. And they aren't that easy to talk about."

He studied her. Finally, he nodded. "I get that too. I've made some mistakes and have things that have happened to me that are hard to talk about. Hard to think about, too."

A cowboy leading his horse behind him walked past them. Dalton reached out protectively, took her arm and moved her over a step, getting her out of the pathway. His touch was gentle and reminded her again that he was always being protective of her. So unlike any of the other men who'd been in her life…not that he was in her life in that way. But she knew she was starting to wish deep down inside that he was.

What would it be like to be loved by this gentle, protective man?

"This isn't really the place to talk about it but, I'd like to."

"What if I come by tonight after the rodeo when the kids are asleep?"

She smiled. Her spirits lifted more than she wanted to acknowledge. "That would be good. You've caught on quick that it's not always easy to have a conversation when little kids are around."

Dalton's smile was as heart-stopping as it got. "I've noticed."

"Then I'll see you in a bit."

He tipped his hat and her heart stuttered in her chest. She managed a small smile and then turned and went back into the building. She had committed to telling her story to Dalton.

And she was resigned to the fact that he would either understand…or he wouldn't.

CHAPTER TEN

Rae Anne left the rodeo soon after speaking with Dalton. It was nine when she gathered up Joey and headed home. He chattered all the way home about the cowboys and the animals until he fell asleep right in the middle of talking.

Adela was rocking Grace when Rae Anne carried Joey inside. She put him in bed and then came back and took the baby.

"She was adorable." Adela smiled sweetly. "I tried not to hold her the whole time, but it's hard not to."

"I know. I have to make myself give her time in

the crib too. But since she's my last one, I've given myself permission to enjoy her babyhood and not worry about if I'm spoiling her."

"She's very blessed to have you as a mother. I'll be going. Have a lovely night, dear."

"Thank you so much for watching her."

"Any time." She gathered up her purse and then paused before heading to the door to place a gentle hand on Rae Anne's arm. "You do know that if you need help in any way…or to just talk about something going on in your life, we're here to help."

"I know. And I'm very grateful."

After Adela left, Rae Anne sat down in the rocker beside the window and cuddled Grace as she watched for Dalton's truck lights to appear down the drive. It didn't take long for her sweet child to drift off to sleep. Looking down into her tiny face, Rae Anne didn't think she could ever survive putting her baby in harm's way. And that was what she needed to explain to Dalton.

She gently placed the baby in the crib and then headed to the kitchen when headlights flashed across the living room. Dalton was here.

Instead of trepidation at seeing him and telling him about her sordid past, she was startled to feel heat flush her cheeks and the excited rush of adrenaline hit her blood in anticipation of seeing him.

The knock at the door reminded her that she had to move, had to open the door if she was ever going to see him or expose her most hideous secrets to Dalton.

That thought alone doused the anticipation because once he knew, he would probably lose any kind of respect that he might have held for her. *Don't tell him.*

Ignoring the voice in her head, she stalked to the door and swung it open with the determination to do the right thing.

The startled look on Dalton's face told her she might have been a little too aggressive.

"Well, hey there," he drawled. "Are you about to run from a fire or something?" He looked past her into the house. "If so, you're forgetting your kids."

What a man. Even while teasing her, he thought of her children. Butterflies erupted inside her. "No, I'm sorry. I'm forcing myself to do this so I guess I got a little carried away—oh never mind. Do you want to talk inside or outside?"

"How about out here so you don't have to worry about Joey overhearing."

"That would be great. Do you want something to drink?"

"Nope. Just some facts. And if you're having to force yourself—" He was watching her and she felt as if he could see every corner of her soul.

"I want to tell you. I just fear what you'll think of me." *There—it was out there.* She let out a long breath of air and walked out onto the front porch. The coyotes could be heard in the distance. She'd grown used to hearing them and no longer felt a pang of alarm when they seemed closer than other times. She sat on swing and he leaned against the porch railing. They seemed to always be on her porch.

"So, I guess there's nothing to do but tell you."

"That works for me. Like I said, only if you're sure you want to tell me."

"I do. You deserve to know. I wasn't married to

Joey's father and he wasn't interested in marriage when I met him. He disappeared out of my life about as fast as a snake in tall grass. He wasn't even interested in being listed on the birth certificate. But I did it anyway, thinking Joey had a right to have who his daddy is listed on it. And I also felt like Jacob should help with child support." She paused, remembering all the months of her pregnancy that she'd worried over what to do and what she felt was best for Joey. "Jacob, to his credit, agreed to the child support without me having to bring charges or anything. But to this day he hasn't seen his son."

Dalton's expression turned to disgust. "So Joey hasn't ever been in contact with his dad?"

"No. I'm embarrassed to admit that I had really poor judgment where Jacob was concerned. He turned out to not be the man that I thought he was. Yes, Joey has a dad listed on his birth certificate but that's all he has." She cringed telling him this, exposing her bad judgment. Her mistakes. Her throat was scratchy and she softly cleared it. "It appears that my judgment of men just grew worse rather than lesson learned. I met

Reese about a year after Joey was born." Her stomach clenched despite not having seen any condemnation in Dalton's eyes. *Well, one mistake could be overlooked. But two?*

"And that would be Grace's dad?"

She nodded. "He was nice and fun and paid attention to my little boy, who'd never had much attention from a male. I hadn't dated since Jacob and hadn't planned to date at all, but Reese was nice. And persistent since he lived in the condo across from mine. I saw him a lot. He started inviting me out to lunch. I worked my job at the nursing home while I was building up my client list online with my author assistant business. He never seemed to mind that Joey was on our lunch dates and it even seemed to please him. I never thought anything about the stops he made while we were in the car with him. He was just so genuinely nice, and I was lonely. And I fell for him."

Dalton hadn't moved the whole time she talked until now, and he straightened, no longer leaning against the railing. Instead, he moved to sit in the swing beside her. She felt his presence with every fiber of her body. It was like nothing she'd ever experienced before.

"You loved him?"

"I thought I did. But again, it turns out that I didn't know him. He'd always said he was in the import/export business. He worked from home and I could tell that whatever he did, he did well. Turns out he imported and exported drugs."

Dalton's expression darkened. "What a jerk," he muttered, angrily. "What did you do when you found out?"

"I didn't know what to do at first. I found out that I was a cover for him. Me and my son. He made drops and contacts while we were in the car with him. I even made a few drops for him and didn't realize what I was delivering."

"You're kidding?"

"Sadly, no. He asked me to deliver a box to a business; it was supposed to be parts for a collectible car. I did it a few times. I was so furious when I found out what he was doing. I had put my son in jeopardy. I only found out what was going on when a narcotics cop approached me and told me. I made a deal with them, turned him in and then went into hiding until I testified against him. He went to jail, and was supposed to spend time in prison… I had made a complete mess of my life. And of my children's." She looked down at her clasped hands and the shame that hung over her like a dark cloud felt as heavy as concrete.

Dalton's gentle hand rested on her shoulder. "You didn't know."

"I realize that but I feel like I should have known something. How could I have spent time with him…married him? I lived with him, for goodness' sakes, and I never caught on to the fact that something was horribly wrong? I'm not a complete dope."

"No, you're not. He must have been a great deceiver."

"Still, it gives me no relief knowing this. And it doesn't help me now."

"So what about now? Why are you on the run?"

"Because, about three weeks ago I found out that he'd cut a deal and was going to be released. He agreed to testify against some of the bigger bosses in the organization. He's getting out. I didn't know what to do. I panicked. I knew that he knew he'd been caught because of me. I had divorced him immediately and I was afraid he might come after me. But I was also afraid he might come after Grace. I didn't put him down as the father of Grace, and I don't think with his record he could have any claim on her but still, I'm worried about him finding out and showing up. I don't want him to even look at her."

"I don't blame you. It sounds like you might need to worry that he could harm you and your children."

She nodded. That thought was the main reason she'd told Dalton. She needed someone else to know. "I have a feeling in my gut that he's going to come after me. Sweet Mr. Overton kept asking me what was wrong. That man might be old but he was perceptive and knew I was afraid. He told me he knew something was wrong and if I ever needed somewhere to go that he had a place. He said he would never use it again and I was more than welcome to use it for as long as I needed. I took him up on his offer."

"And ended up in a flood and in labor."

"Yes," she whispered, watching him.

How would he react to all that she'd said?

"Why wouldn't you tell me this before now?"

She stood and moved to the railing. Her hands gripped the edges of the wood as she stared out across the darkness. "Because I just feel so dirty when I think about him. And I feel ashamed. And really stupid—I hate that word and that feeling."

Dalton came to stand behind her. She could feel his body heat and the scent of maleness and leather drifted to her. He tugged her around to look at him. "Listen to me. You have nothing to feel bad about. Release it."

Shame came over her and tears welled up in her eyes. "I can't do that. It's so embarrassing that I could have fallen twice into relationships with men who I thought were good guys. How can a mother with a good head on her shoulders do such a thing?" The question ate at her night and day.

Looking at Dalton, she just wanted to climb into a hole—she was so embarrassed that her judgment was so horrible. He had to think badly of her. *How could he not?*

Dalton had been shocked to his core by the things Rae Anne told him. She did appear to be a smart woman with a good head on her shoulders so he couldn't help but be baffled by her bad choices. Did loneliness do that to a person? Or love?

He wanted to throttle the two men.

Lifting his hand, he ran his fingertips gently down her cheek and picked the tears up with his knuckle and traced the curve of her face. "You didn't deserve this."

She had gone very still; her downcast eyes avoided his. He felt the warmth of her breath against his fingers as he gently took her face between his hands and tilted her head up so she had to look at him. It struck him as their gazes locked that he wanted to be the man who didn't let her down. He wanted to be the man in her life who wasn't a mistake.

"Rae Anne," he said softly. He lowered his head and captured her lips with his.

Warm and soft and salty with her tears, her lips accepted his but he felt her tense and immediately he stopped kissing her and just pulled her close, wanting to comfort her right now. But he knew he could have kept kissing her forever. The beating of her heart against his felt almost like one heart beating. "They didn't deserve you," he said gently, into her hair. "And they're the losers where the babies are concerned."

The tension eased at his words. "I think so. Thank you for saying that," she whispered against his shoulder as her arms came around him.

He felt the hesitancy in her actions and it made him want to hold her longer, but almost immediately she slipped out of his arms.

"I can't afford another misstep, Dalton. You should know that I'm not open to another relationship. I've got two babies now and I don't need anything in my life but them. I can't allow myself to feel this…"

He knew what "this" meant. Because he felt it too. It was strong and powerful and filled him with longings he'd never felt before. He knew in his heart that he didn't deserve it. He had his own demons to fight. His own reasons for not feeling as if he deserved to be loved.

"It won't happen again." She was right. She'd probably be horrified when she found out that he'd been involved in a wreck that had taken a mother and child's life. He couldn't think about it and he certainly couldn't talk about it. She'd had enough men in her life who didn't deserve her. He didn't either.

She watched him, as if trying to assess whether she could trust what he was saying. At last she gave a nod. "Okay. Thank you for understanding."

What looked like worry crinkled her brow and he wanted to smooth it away. Felt compelled to give her a champion. She and her babies deserved a man who could come in and be there for them. Someone who would take up for them instead of tear them down.

She tore her gaze away from his and strode to the edge of the porch. The moonlight caressed her silhouette. She was beautiful in a soft, feminine way that could very easily drive him crazy.

"So what's going to happen if this man shows up wanting to see his daughter?"

"I'm not going to let him near her. The only way he could prove she was his is with a DNA test. But I don't think he would go through that. He doesn't want a child." Her voice wobbled. "If he shows up here, he's looking for revenge and that's the only reason he'll show up. If he wants Grace, it will be because he wants to pay me back for putting him in prison. And that's what terrifies me."

Dalton knew that Rae Anne wasn't as gullible as she felt she was. This guy had to have really pulled the wool over her eyes for her to not see at least some hint of the man he really was. And that meant he was a calculating manipulator along with being a drug dealer. "I hate to agree but you're probably right. We need to tell Brady Cannon, the sheriff. He and his department need to be aware of what's going on."

"I don't think there's anything they can do right now."

"Look, Amber had a stalker when she first came

here and Chase got Brady involved. It just makes good sense to let him know what might be coming."

"No one knows I'm here. I just left. I told a couple of friends I was leaving, but didn't even tell them where I was going."

"What if he checks hospitals?"

Her expression tensed. "I'm trying not to think about that. I just get mad thinking about it. That man cannot find us and that's all there is to it. I'll…I'll leave before he does."

"Tell Brady, okay? It's going to be alright."

She didn't look completely convinced but she nodded. "Okay, I'll tell him."

He smiled at her. "There you go. You made it through a lot more in the last few weeks than most people would have been able to handle. You can handle this too."

"I just get overwhelmed if I let myself get caught up in how badly I've messed things up and what it could cost my children as they grow up without a dad. Thanks for your support."

"Thanks for trusting me. I'm going to head out now. Try to get some rest. I'll talk to you tomorrow."

He turned and headed for his truck. She stood on the porch and watched him as he drove away.

It was one of the hardest things he'd ever done.

CHAPTER ELEVEN

The next morning, determined to move forward with her life, and needing a distraction from the brief kiss that she'd shared with Dalton, Rae Anne pushed the stroller through the large open doorway of Pete's Feed and Seed. The kiss had been brief but potent. It had taken her by surprise that he kissed her. She could almost believe that it had been out of comfort only but that would be a lie. The air had shifted the instant his lips had touched hers, like the charge in the air after a direct strike of lightning. Her knees had gone weak—she forced the memory from her mind and focused on her surroundings.

The scent of grain hung heavy in the air of the building that was packed with every imaginable thing a rancher or farmer might need: pet supplies, cattle and horse medicines, colorful rain gauges, and more. Joey immediately started reaching for items from his position in the front of the stroller. It was built for two, with its place at the back for the baby and at the front—close to everything—for her busy toddler.

"Whoa there, little man." She pulled a gauge that looked like a sunflower from his grasp.

"He can't hurt it," a tall man with a balding head and a kind face said from behind the counter. "I'm Pete and if there's anything I can help you with, I'd be happy to. You must be the new addition to town from out at the Overton place."

Rae Anne introduced herself. "It's a pleasure to meet you. And I'm not so sure you completely understand the power of a three-year-old with busy hands." She laughed and handed the rain gauge to Pete.

"I want out, Mama," Joey exclaimed, looking around at the store. She could only imagine what all he could get into in the store. There was stuff hanging everywhere: bridles, brushes, rain gauges, ropes—just an array of things that would catch a little boy's attention.

"No, you need to stay in the stroller." Trying to take a three-year-old out and an infant made keeping up with them a lot harder. She couldn't let him roam free.

Disappointment wrinkled his little brow. He strained in the stroller seat.

Pete came around the counter and held out a purple lollypop. "How about a pop?" He grinned and instantly Joey's stricken expression turned into a smile.

"Say thank you," Rae Anne prompted him as he took the sucker. He eagerly plopped the sucker into his mouth.

"No sir. I said tell Mr. Pete thank you or give the sucker back."

Joey immediately told Pete thank-you and continued enjoying the candy.

"So what can I do for you?" the storeowner asked, his eyes twinkling.

"I'd like some of those plants you have out front." She loved flowers and just hadn't had a place to grow them for a long time. "I've never had room to grow my own tomatoes and really want to try." Plus, she really needed something to keep her occupied and Joey would enjoy it too. He loved to be outside and so a garden made perfect sense. She did most of her work at night after the children were in bed. Being a virtual assistant for authors was a solitary job that required a lot of computer time compiling spreadsheets, formatting books, and a host of other things her clients might need. It kept her busy and now that she wasn't working at the nursing home any longer, she was trying to find more clients through recommendations of her other ones.

She was still shocked and forever grateful that Grace was a good sleeper. Joey had been a restless sleeper and had never gotten on a regular schedule. He had been overactive from the moment he was conceived. The little toot was going to be a football player or soccer player for certain.

"Let's go see what you want then."

She followed Pete outside to where a great array of healthy flowers and vegetable seedlings were stacked on racks. It was a beautiful spring morning and the town was busy. Trucks and trailers moved down Main Street in the tiny, colorful town.

Every wooden building along Main Street was painted in colorful colors. Heavenly Inspirations Hair Salon was across the street and it was a very pretty pink. There was a purple building and a blue building among others. It was happy.

And despite the things going on in her life, she felt happy looking around this town.

This was a great place.

She needed to call tomorrow and check on Mr. Overton and let him know how they were doing. And to thank him and express how very grateful she was for him letting her use his place.

A real estate office next door to the feed store caught her attention. *It would be so nice to think about settling here.*

But right now she couldn't even think about what tomorrow held for her and her children, much less the future. She was just living moment by moment. The touch of Dalton's lips on hers ambushed her again; butterflies erupted inside her chest.

She tore her gaze away from the real estate office. Her pulse jigged at an erratic pace. She had no room for dreams such as that…none. She had messed up too many times in her life. It still baffled her how quickly Dalton had accepted her mess-ups. He'd not judged her; she'd expected him to think less of her but he didn't seem to.

She focused on the tomato plants.

"Oh." She gasped when she read the tags and saw several varieties: Celebrity, Better Boy, Fat Boy. She looked up at Pete in confusion. "There are so many different kinds."

He grinned and picked up a six-pack of sturdy-looking young plants. "These Celebrity plants grow real well in these parts. That's a good one for you to start with. And how about a couple of the cherry tomatoes? My wife loves to eat them straight off the vine."

"Can I eat 'em off the vine?" Joey asked and Rae

Anne bit back a chuckle because he didn't like tomatoes. But, there was always hope that if he could pull them off the vine, he'd start loving them.

"That sounds wonderful. I'll take them." She felt good about her choices and picked out a few other things. Joey decided they had to grow some squash because he liked the picture. Grace stirred and started to fuss.

"She don't like sittin'." Joey squirmed in the stroller. "Me neither."

Pete chuckled. "You sure have been a good boy in that stroller today."

Joey frowned and crossed his arms, pouting. "I don't like it."

"We're almost ready to go home," she said, as a truck pulled up.

"Norma Sue!" Joey exclaimed gleefully as the rancher woman climbed from the big truck.

She wore her white Stetson and had on jeans and a plaid shirt. "Well howdy there, little pardner," she called, heading his way. "What are y'all doing?" She planted her hands on her hips and stared at the array of plants in their cart.

"We're gonna do a garden," Joey said proudly and then frowned. "I want out."

"You do look a little ragged around the edges." She ruffled his hair. "What if I take him over to grab a breakfast muffin at Sam's while you finish up? You can come join us when you're done shopping."

Rae Anne squinted at her. "Are you sure?"

"Am I sure? Sure I am. Me and my little buddy like hanging out together."

Joey grinned as if he'd just been given the moon and the look almost made Rae Anne tear up. "Will Roy Don and Dalt be there?"

"I don't think so. But some of my other friends will be there." She hiked a questioning brow at Rae Anne.

"Yes, he can go. Thank you for taking him." Within seconds, she'd freed her son from the constraints of the stroller. He immediately took the older woman's hand and they strolled down the plank sidewalk together, talking about muffins. Rae Anne watched as the two went inside the diner a few doors down from the feed store. He was chattering up a storm as the door closed behind them.

This was a good place to raise a little boy.

She could see him here growing up surrounded by open pastures and lots of room to roam. And wonderful, welcoming people like Norma Sue being involved in his life was priceless.

If only she didn't have to worry about the possibility of Grace's father showing up.

Turning back toward the flowers, she saw a broad-shouldered man in starched jeans and a khaki long-sleeved shirt approach them. A badge glinted in the sunlight.

"Hey there, Sheriff," Pete greeted the tough-looking lawman.

"Afternoon, Pete. And you too, miss." He lifted his Stetson from his head momentarily before he returned it back on his dark hair. "I'm Brady Cannon. The sheriff of Mule Hollow. I saw you and your children over here and thought I'd come introduce myself. Are you Rae Anne Tyson? The new lady living in the Overton place?"

Her heart thumped like hail on a tin roof and she wasn't sure why. "Rae—I mean, yes, I'm Rae Anne Tyson." She held out her hand and told herself to stop being nervous. She hadn't done anything wrong. Marrying a drug dealer, divorcing him and having his baby was not the smartest thing she could have done but it wasn't a crime.

"I hear you were very lucky the night you came to town."

"Oh, very lucky. I'm still not able to think about it and not get emotional." She fought off the lump that suddenly clogged her throat. "Dalton was an answer to my prayers."

It was so very true. God had heard her pleas. She just hoped He was still listening and that she was worrying about Reese for nothing.

"Well, I just wanted to welcome you and let you know if you ever need anything, me and my deputies are at your service."

This was her opportunity to tell him.

To do as she'd told Dalton she would do and let the sheriff know she was afraid trouble might follow her to this tiny town. “Thank you. I’ll remember that.” She couldn’t tell him.

Because she hoped with all her heart that she never had to ask him for help.

CHAPTER TWELVE

"Dalton."

"What?" Dalton glanced at Treb.

Treb's lip hitched into a half grin. "Don't shoot the messenger. I've called your name three times. You were deep in thought. I recon she must have been real interesting to have caught your attention like that."

"And how do you know I was thinking about a woman?"

Treb chuckled and hung a wrist over his saddle horn. "Believe me, it was pretty obvious. I've seen many a Marine with that look on their face while reading a message from home."

Dalton frowned. He didn't want to discuss Rae Anne with anyone. He had her on his mind, though, and there was no getting away from her. That kiss…man, that kiss had tore him up. It was all he could think about. Brief but powerful in a way that dug deeper than anything he'd ever felt.

It had shaken him and startled him that she had two babies by different fathers and one of them was a convicted drug dealer. That was so off the mark from what he'd have ever thought she was going to tell him last night. *How on earth had a woman like Rae Anne fallen for those guys? Especially a creep like her ex?* It just didn't make sense to him.

No, there was no way he could tell Treb or even any of his partners about her problems; that was her business. It was her story to tell or not tell. But the fact that she'd chosen to tell him meant a lot.

"Yeah, I can't imagine how hard it must be for all the service men to be away from their loved ones."

Treb looked thoughtful for a moment. "It was

hard, but you do what you have to do."

Dalton didn't miss the shadow that crossed his expression and he wondered what Treb's story was. He knew that before he'd joined the Marines that he'd been on the rodeo circuit and highly ranked in the standings. But that's all Dalton knew. That and he liked and respected him. Treb had been a hard worker from the moment he'd shown up and signed on with them. New Horizon Ranch was benefiting from a cowboy of his caliber working on the ranch.

As if on cue, Treb pointed to a heifer. "I was just going to ask if you noticed that heifer has an ulcer on its leg."

Dalton glanced toward the small heifer Treb pointed at. "No, I didn't see that." He hated to admit that he'd been that lost in thought. It was a bad sore.

"Want me to pull it out of the group?"

"Yeah, do that and we'll take a closer look."

"Will do." Treb eased his horse into the crowding herd so that he could cut the heifer from the rest.

Dalton watched him work. He'd told them he'd

been raised on a ranch and it was obvious. Yanking his thoughts back to his work, Dalton urged his horse forward and drove the cattle toward the pens.

He'd been a cowboy since the day he'd been born. His dad had him in the saddle riding with him before he was one. He'd been riding in the saddle alone by the time he was three and working cattle with the men by the age of five. For an active kid like him, it had been a great thing. He loved this life, his passion and after the wreck, it had saved his life.

Now it was all he had.

All he'd ever let himself have. And he'd made it. Until last night.

Until he'd kissed Rae Anne. Until he'd realized that he could have strong feelings for her and her children.

Dalton reined up on his horse, bringing it to a halt, and stared at the cattle moving along in front of him. He'd never felt what he felt when he'd kissed her, when he held her. But if he was any kind of man, he'd stop thinking about her, about the kiss. He'd stop thinking about a life and the possibility of a future with her. And her family.

He didn't deserve a family of his own.

They didn't need him for anything other than to make sure they were safe. And that was something he planned to make certain of.

He'd do everything in his power to make certain that her ex wasn't going to harm her.

Tomorrow he'd talk to Brady and find out what kind of rights the drug dealer had. He was fairly certain he had none but if he was angry enough at Rae Anne for testifying against him, then there was no telling what he might do.

Suddenly Dalton couldn't stop thinking about it. He turned his horse and urged him into a lope. "Hey, Treb," he called as he passed him. "I've got to get back. You alright here?"

"I'm fine. I've got this," Treb called, but Dalton was already urging his horse into a gallop.

He needed to find out where the thug was. Hopefully she was right and no one knew where to find her. That would at least give them some time.

By the time she got home from the morning outing to Mule Hollow, it was lunch time. Rae Anne got the babies fed and then rocked Grace to sleep while Joey played cars on the floor. He was chattering up a storm about the two older men playing checkers at the diner. They had been fairly funny while they sat there at the front window playing. Joey had loved watching them and giggled several times when they teased him.

After Grace fell asleep, she lay her in the crib and then read a story to Joey and put him down for a nap. Immediately she went to the phone to call the nursing home and asked her friend Desi to let her talk to Mr. Overton.

"Rae Anne, he's not really feeling good today. He's been lying down all day."

He was amazing for his age but he did have bad days where he just seemed to run out of steam and he didn't seem to remember as well as other days.

"Where did you disappear to anyway?" Desi asked.

The question put Rae Anne in a hard spot. She didn't want to lie to her friend but she also wasn't willing to tell even a friend where she was. It was just too risky. "I just had to leave town. Listen, could you tell Mr. O that I called to check on him? Tell him we're doing good and I'll call again soon."

"I don't know why you're so secretive but I'll tell him." There was no mistaking that Desi was aggravated.

"Thanks, Desi. I owe you. That's just all I can say right now. Okay?"

"Fine. I know you have your reasons. If you need me, I'm here. Have you had your baby yet?"

Feeling so very torn, Rae Anne had to tell the truth. "I had her the day I left. She's doing great, though."

"Are you kidding me!" Desi exclaimed, making Rae Anne feel all the more as though she'd been careless. "Are you okay?"

"I'm good. I really am. Look, Desi, I have to go but I'm telling the truth. Everything is fine. I promise."

"Fine. But you running away like that wasn't normal. I know something is going on."

"Desi, has anyone come by looking for me?" *There, she'd asked.*

"No, but I have a feeling you're about to tell me there might be someone doing just that."

"Maybe. And the thing is, I really don't need him to know where I've gone. It's easier if you don't know anything. Okay?"

"Fine. But if you think for one minute that I'd tell someone something you don't want them to know, then you're wrong."

"It's not that. I don't think that at all. This is just the way it needs to be."

"Alright then, but girl, you keep safe and call when you can."

"I will." Rae Anne said good-bye and set her phone down on the table. She walked over to the kitchen window and stared out at the pastures. Bending her head, she prayed that God would make all her worries be for nothing. That Reese would have other things besides her to worry about and that they'd be safe here.

A knock on the front door caused her to jump.

She walked through the house and glanced out the window beside the front door. Dalton and Sheriff Brady stood on the porch.

What?

She fumbled to get the door opened, her fingers suddenly not working right. Her mouth went dry and the pit of her stomach felt hollowed out. "Hi," she said, breathless as her nerves frazzled within her. "Is something wrong?"

Dalton's expression was tense. "I brought Brady out to talk to you."

Brady removed his hat. "Dalton explained what was going on with your ex-husband and I thought it would be a good idea to talk." The sheriff looked about as strong and capable as any law enforcement officer she'd ever seen. But that was beside the point as she glared at Dalton.

"You told him. Dalton, this is my business—" she started to say, trying to control her anger. He had no right to tell the sheriff about this. Even if he had rescued her and her family from those floodwaters, he'd overstepped the boundaries.

Unfazed by her anger, he said, "You're going to want to hear what he has to say. Can you come out here?"

She crossed her arms and struggled to compose herself as she stepped out onto the porch, glancing back to make certain Joey wasn't up. He hadn't been napping long so they should be okay. The last thing she wanted was for him to find a sheriff on the porch or to overhear this conversation. The poor kid had been uprooted from his home and was adjusting well despite all the reasons he should be traumatized. He didn't need more added to that.

"What can I do for you?" she asked the sheriff.

He smiled kindly. He was a handsome man, a giant of a man. He had to be six foot five inches at least.

"I realize you might not want to have this information public and you can rest assured that it's safe with me. Only my deputy Zane Cantrell knows about this. He's an ex-Texas Ranger and was heavily involved in the WITSEC program."

"Excuse me, the what?"

"The witness protection program. After hearing your story, we did some checking and found out that your ex entered the program, as we suspected he would. He ratted out some pretty big names. His life isn't worth much on the street any longer."

Rae Anne felt faint.

Dalton was at her side instantly. "Hold on there." He held her up. "Are you okay?"

She tried to speak but nothing came out. She took a deep breath and then tried again. Turmoil churned inside her. She was disappointed in Reese and felt completely betrayed by him but she'd never wish harm to him. "This is terrible."

"Yes, he's in a lot of trouble. And I suspect you

made a wise decision leaving town. You might not have any contact with him but they don't know that. They could suspect you know where he's hiding and that makes it very dangerous for you."

"Great. Just great." She dropped her forehead to her palm and rubbed her brow. *How could she have done this to her children?* She was the worst mother in the world. And now, she felt weak and helpless. And she despised feeling that way almost as much as she hated feeling like a fool.

"You'll be safe here," Sheriff Brady offered. "If you're sure you haven't left a trail of any kind. I'd suggest not contacting anyone from back home. I suspect your ex is going to be too busy looking over his shoulder to worry about finding you."

"Are you sure?"

He nodded. "And even if I'm wrong, you're in a good place. We look out for each other here. If this guy decides to cut ties with the WITSEC program and come looking for you, he's signing his own death warrant and I doubt he'll do that. But if he does, Zane's people will let him know the instant he does it."

"So I'm hoping you can relax now." Dalton's gaze locked with hers. "You deserve some time with your new baby that has no fear attached to it. Think you can do that?"

He'd done this for her and she'd almost gotten angry at him. Not that she wanted him to keep stepping across boundaries but… "Thank you." Her voice shook as relief hit her. She could let her guard down. She could stop thinking about picking up and running again.

At least for now anyway.

CHAPTER THIRTEEN

Dalton didn't think he would ever forget the look on Rae Anne's face when she realized that she and her children were safe. At least for now. It was a mixture of joy and relief and he could tell by her voice that there was disbelief there too. And tears.

Those tears had cut straight to his heart. The fact that she'd had so much fear weighing on her hurt him.

He walked Brady out to his truck but his mind was on Rae Anne as he held his hand out and shook Brady's hand. "Thanks for coming. If you hear anything to the contrary of what we just told her, I'd appreciate you letting me know."

"I'll do it. But like I said, he'd be a fool to come out of hiding to find her. Her instincts to come here served her well, I think."

Dalton agreed but his instinct told him he needed to stay on his toes.

She was still on the porch when he turned back. "Hopefully you can relax even a little bit now. I was wondering if you might want to bring Joey over and let him sit on a horse. I can work with him a bit and lead him around the arena. I think he'll like it."

Her eyes lit up. "He'll love it. I think that's the perfect way to celebrate." She looked as if she was lost for a moment and then she engulfed him in a hard hug. "I'm sorry. I was so angry with you for sharing my info with the sheriff. You're a good man, Dalton. You've done so much for my family. If there is anything I can ever do for you, please let me know." She pulled back and looked up at him in earnest.

His heart ached as he looked at her. He wanted her to throw herself back into his arms and to replay that kiss that had not diminished in his mind. "I'm glad. I just want you safe and happy." He snagged his hat off his head and held it in both of his hands. *Better that than reach out and pull her back to him.* "Rae Anne, I hope you know you deserve much more than you've had where men are concerned. And that includes me. I just want you to know that."

"Right now, I don't want to think about my foolish mistakes. I want to think about the freedom to enjoy the next little while with my babies. Not having to look over my shoulder is such an amazing relief." She laughed suddenly and a smile like none he'd seen before spread across her beautiful face. "It truly is a new beginning. I can't wait to tell Joey we're coming over to ride a horse. I hope you're prepared for an excited little boy?"

Dalton couldn't speak… Dear Lord in heaven, he was in trouble as he stared at her with that smile and those twinkling eyes.

"I'll see you later," he said gruffly. "When you're ready. Just come on over anytime." And then he planted his hat on his head and barreled toward his truck. He didn't even shoot her a glance as the engine roared to life. If he looked at her right now, he'd be racing back over there, hauling her into his arms and planting his lips to hers.

And that would not be good…oh, it would be good. Great.

Amazing.

But it wouldn't be good for Rae Anne.

She deserved better than she'd had and that meant he had to figure out a man for her and steer her toward him. An honorable man. A strong man to keep her safe.

One who could protect her and give her everything she deserved.

He didn't know who that was yet—but he did know it wasn't him.

Treb came to mind…maybe Treb. He was a great guy, a military man, which was perfect. The problem was, Dalton immediately wanted to hit something just from thinking about a man other than him being with Rae Anne.

And that was another problem.

An hour later, Rae Anne drove up to the huge stone house of the New Horizon Ranch. She saw several trucks parked at the house. The side of the house faced the parking area and there was a patio that wrapped around to the side and expanded into a large terrace at the back that overlooked rolling pastures. A small crowd was gathered on the terrace.

The partners were all here.

Maddie waved at her as she broke away from the group and came her way. Rae Anne didn't see Dalton and though excited to see the group, she was disappointed that he wasn't among them.

She had hugged him on impulse earlier and had wanted to hold onto him forever.

The realization had startled her. And though she knew she'd had bad judgment before—she knew Dalton Borne was the kind of man to hold onto for life…if a woman were so lucky to get the opportunity.

"Hey there," Maddie greeted them. She picked Joey up and held him on her hip. "Good to see you made it." Maddie smiled at her and then looked at Joey. "Little buddy, I hear you're fixin' to ride a horse."

"Dalt's gonna ride me on it. I'm a big boy."

Maddie grinned. "Yes you are. And when you're done, you can ask your mom if y'all can eat dinner with all of us."

"Can we, Mama?"

"We would love to." Rae Anne felt excited once more about the friends they were making here. "Thanks for asking us. Is Dalton around?"

"He's in the barn, getting the horse ready. What if I watch Grace while you take Joey to ride?"

"That would be nice. If you're sure."

"I'm more than sure. I'm so looking forward to having a baby of my own. I can't wait." She set Joey back on his feet. "Okay, buddy, it's time for you to go meet Dalton. He's waiting on you."

Joey got a darling, serious look on his tiny face.

"I'm ready to ride."

Rae Anne handed Grace over to Maddie and the diaper bag. "Her bottle is in there if she gets fussy. But she just ate so she should be fine. Come get me if you need me. And thank you, again."

Maddie stared down at the baby and sighed. "She's just so precious. Thank you for letting me watch her. Cliff and I are trying to have our own baby but so far we just haven't been successful. I keep telling myself it will happen in God's timing but I'm getting a little anxious. So I'm loving the idea of babysitting." She smiled heartily at Rae Anne. "Now go have fun."

"Thanks and I'll be praying you get your baby soon."

"Much appreciated." Maddie headed toward the house, cooing to Grace and lost in her own little world.

Rae Anne took Joey's hand and led him across the parking area to the stable that Maddie had pointed out to them. There were several, so she hadn't been certain where to go.

The grassy scent of hay greeted them, along with

the soft nicker of the horses that looked at them from across metal gates. Joey was in awe as he stared at each one. She was too. The place was very nice, with a wide concrete alley flanked on both sides by a long row of stalls. Dalton was in a stall near the middle of the building and Joey spotted him immediately.

Rae Anne's stomach tipped to the side when he turned and met her gaze. She suddenly felt as if she were riding over the highest rise of a roller coaster—the world fell away and she lost her breath.

"Hey there." His eyes warmed, as if he felt it too. Then he focused on Joey. "Glad you came. You ready to ride Trigger?"

"Yes." Joey, without fear, marched toward the horse.

"Whoa." Dalton halted him and crouched down to his level. "Hold on. First, never approach a horse alone. Let me introduce you."

Joey nodded, his eyes glued to Dalton with hero worship written all over him. He was soaking up everything Dalton said. Rae Anne watched as Dalton introduced Joey to the beautiful sandy-toned horse and Joey laughed when it wagged its head up and down at him several times.

Rae Anne held back as Dalton took Joey's hand and together they led the horse out to the arena.

She wasn't even nervous when Dalton lifted Joey and set him in the saddle—which was a shock considering she wasn't all that comfortable at the thought of getting on one. But this was Dalton and she knew he would take care of her baby. The expression on her little boy's face was priceless. And Dalton's was too as he looked sweetly at Joey.

"I've gotcha, little man," he said, and she knew he did. "You're going to be a regular cowboy in no time at all."

Rae Anne's heart clutched as her breath caught with emotion. She would forever love this man who had been so important to them since the night of the flood.

"I'm doin' it, Dalt! Mama, I'm riding. Dalt's got me though, so don't worry none. Okay?"

"You're looking great. And I'm not worried at all."

And she wasn't. She knew that as long as he was with Dalton, he was safe.

Dalton led Joey around on the horse at a very slow and easy pace and he enjoyed the enthusiasm the little fella had at being there. Dalton had been tense since he'd left Rae Anne's house earlier that day and now he made himself relax.

After Joey had made several trips around the arena on the horse, he crooked his finger at Rae Anne, who stood beside the arena gate watching them. "Come over here."

She walked across the soft dirt and stopped a couple of feet from him.

"How would you like to ride?"

Her brow knitted. "I've never ridden. Let Joey. I wouldn't want to take his time."

He couldn't believe it. "You live in Texas and you've never ridden a horse? That's a shame and we need to fix that. You need to ride. You need to know what Joey is experiencing."

"Ride, Mama. It's *fun!*"

She laughed at Joey's enthusiasm; her hesitancy disappeared. "It does look fun."

"Joey, you want to get down and watch Mom ride?"

When Joey grinned and nodded, Dalton reached up and lifted the boy down. "Go sit by the gate there and watch your mama, okay?" Joey happily did as he was asked and ran over to the spot and sat down cross-legged, planting his elbows on his knees and his chin in his palm as he watched them.

Rae Anne looked nervous again. "Hey, don't look so nervous."

"Is it that obvious?"

"The fact that you're a little green is a clue that you've either eaten something that's not agreeing with you or you're really nervous."

Her brows crinkled over alarmed eyes. "That bad?"

He laughed. "Naw, I just wanted to loosen you up. You're as beautiful as ever—just a bit pale."

She looked startled and he wasn't sure whether it was at the compliment or the fact that he had said it.

"Why do you look so shocked? You are, you know."

"Thank you, but we both know that's stretching the truth—and that is *not* my attempt at fishing for more compliments—"

He couldn't believe it; she really didn't know how beautiful she was. No, she wasn't a classic glamour beauty, but she was more…there was just a soft quality about her that he couldn't look away from. "I think you're about the most beautiful woman I've ever seen. And you can't say anything to change my mind…" He paused, so tempted to brush his lips across hers. Her eyes drifted to his lips, as if she were wishing… "Um, are you ready?" he asked, needing to stop thinking about what he was thinking about.

Her gaze jerked from his lips to his eyes. "I'm ready."

Something dug deep into his chest.

"I do need to experience this," she said in a rush. "So what do I do?"

"You're frightened, I can tell that and I'm proud of you for overcoming it by riding. But you let me put Joey on this horse and you didn't say anything about being so afraid. Weren't you worried or scared for him?"

Her lips curved gently. "I trusted you. I knew you wouldn't let anything happen to him. And that's the only reason I'm going to get in that saddle myself."

Her words grabbed him right in the heart and squeezed with both hands. "Thanks. Because I wouldn't let anything happen to you or him."

"I know."

"Ride, Mama!" Joey hollered from where he sat. He grinned like a kid in a candy store.

"I think that's my cue."

"Yes. Reach up there and grab that saddle horn and hold on while you put your foot in the stirrup. I'll give you a hand if you need it. Wait, are you up to this?

I mean, you just had a baby."

"It's been nearly a month. I think I'm okay. I'll let you know if I can't do it. I mean, I'd at least like to ride in a small circle so Joey can see me do it."

"Okay, we can do that."

She did as he'd told her and he stood by, holding the reins ready to catch her if she needed his help. She didn't. She settled into the saddle and looked down at him as if she'd done this many times before.

"So far so good." She laughed nervously and glanced at Joey, who clapped for her. She gave the little boy a thumbs-up and he copied her.

Dalton rubbed Trigger's forelock and watched Rae Anne. "Okay, this will be an easy, slow walk. Ready?"

She nodded. "Ready."

He led her around three times at a very easy walk and she smiled the whole time.

"I think I could enjoy this."

"Good. I'm here to help anytime you want lessons. You or Joey," he assured her. They walked around a couple more times and then he brought Trigger to a halt. "Next time I'll hand you the reins. You did great. Maybe we'll go for a ride in the pasture sometime."

"Maybe."

He chuckled at that and reached up to help her dismount. She had almost made it to the ground but her foot slipped in the stirrup and she lost her balance. He caught her in his arms.

"Gotcha." He looked into her wide eyes. She felt light in his arms. "Feels like the first time I met you."

"I hope I'm a little lighter than that first time," she murmured.

He had that urge to kiss her again.

It was an urge that wasn't going away anytime soon.

"I didn't happen to notice your weight when I carried you last time. Or this time either."

"Oh, now that is the perfect answer, cowboy."

He set her on her feet. "I try."

"Mama!" Joey ran up and grabbed her around the legs. "You did it. I so proud of you!"

She looked down at Joey and placed her hand on

his head. “Thank you. And I’m proud of you.”

Dalton wanted her for himself. It was a burning need inside him that suddenly radiated through his soul. He led Trigger toward the gate and fought to get his head back where it needed to be. It was time to eat dinner and try to put distance between him and Rae Anne.

CHAPTER FOURTEEN

All during the evening meal, Rae Anne couldn't shake the feeling that Dalton had withdrawn from her. She tried to mark it off as her imagination at first because when they got back to the house, he went to hang out with the guys around the big BBQ pit while she went to the kitchen to see whether she could help. But everything was already done, so she just visited with Mia, Amber, Maddie, and Sadie. They were having a good time playing with Grace as they took turns cuddling the baby.

"We gather the ride went well," Mia commented, a

twinkle in her gaze.

"Yes, great. Joey loved every moment."

"How about you?" Sadie had her long cinnamon-colored hair pulled into a soft twist on top of her head, which seemed to accentuate her big green eyes and the blatant curiosity sparkling there.

Amber and Maddie looked just as curious.

"You do realize he's handsome, single, and a very eligible bachelor?" Amber grinned.

"I enjoyed the ride. Y'all don't need to get started matchmaking, though."

Maddie chuckled. "We can't help it. We love Dalton. He's very…apart, though. We think he needs someone."

Rae Anne wasn't ready for all of this. She was just getting used to the idea that she had deep feelings for him and though she was so glad to have these four as friends, she wasn't ready to discuss her love life with them. "Maybe so, but I'm not comfortable talking about this," she said truthfully. "I have a lot going on in my life."

"We know." Mia stood up with Grace in her arms.

"Let's go eat and stop pressing. Y'all know she's going to get plenty of that soon enough."

Rae Anne started to follow Mia out the door. "What did Mia mean by that?" she asked Amber, who was closest to her.

She winked. "The posse has you in their sights…well, they've had Dalton in theirs for a while. He's not shown any interest in anyone, but since he fished you out of that flood, he's been a bit preoccupied with helping you and the kids."

Maddie was behind her. "So be on the ready because they love a good match. We've all been touched in varying degrees by their meddling." She chuckled but no more was said as they were too close to the men by then.

Rae Anne tried not to let this information worry her. Dalton was a grown man, after all. He would probably laugh if he knew some older women had him on their matchmaking radar. She was the same way.

They couldn't make Dalton do something he didn't want to do. The last thing she wanted was for him to feel any kind of pressure where she was concerned.

And goodness knew she didn't need any pressure on her—she'd just gotten rid of a little of it that afternoon. Matchmaking was the last thing she needed.

Dalton had put himself smack in the middle of a personal tribulation. He had to force himself not to stare at Rae Anne all through dinner. But it was hard to keep his eyes off her. She and his partners' women all interacted so well—she fit with the group almost as if she belonged. And he was trying to talk himself out of being crazy about her but he'd sabotaged himself from the moment he'd invited her over so he could put Joey on a horse. He'd realized his mistake in the arena and now he knew it could only get worse.

He needed to introduce her to Treb. She deserved a man like Treb. Her laughter had him glancing her way again. Joey was dancing for the group; the little tyke had some awesome moves for a three-year-old.

"So, what's up with you and Rae Anne?" Chase asked quietly from where he sat next to Dalton.

Dalton shrugged and shot him a quick glance before he scooped up a forkful of beans. “Nothing.”

“And I’m not over the moon in love with my lovely wife Amber.”

Dalton grunted. “That’s a lie. You’re a sap over her.”

“Exactly.” He cocked a sarcastic brow. “You’re crazy about her. I can see it and so can everyone else. Why deny it?”

This was not the conversation that needed to be happening with Rae Anne sitting two chairs down the table from him. He’d chosen this seat so he’d have a bit of space between him and Rae Anne but now he realized he should have picked the far end of the large picnic table so that there was a lot of space between her and himself.

“I have my reasons.” He kept his voice barely above a hiss.

“Well, all I have to say is if your reasons for denying you care for her are valid then you’d better tell your face to straighten up because, buddy, your expression was pretty syrupy a moment ago.”

"Great," Dalton grumbled. He crammed a stuffed jalapeno into his mouth without thinking of the consequences until it was too late. Heat suffused his mouth after the first chew of the fiery pepper. He choked and grabbed for his glass of sweet tea and gulped a huge swig.

"You alright?" Cliff asked from across the table.

Dalton nodded, and took another swig of tea and tried to breathe through his nostrils as he realized all eyes were on him. Finally, he glared down the table at Rafe. "I thought you grilled jalapenos."

Rafe grinned. "I did. I just found some extra hot ones at the market. Pretty spicy, huh?"

"Yeah, just caught me off guard." He recovered with a chuckle, and glanced down the table. "Watch out for the peppers."

"You alright, Dalt?" Joey asked from his chair beside Rae Anne.

"I'm fine but you stay away from Rafe's peppers."

That got laughter. Rae Anne smiled but he saw concern in her eyes.

He liked that concern and that smile far too much.

When dinner was over, Rae Anne gathered up her crew and thanked everyone for a wonderful evening. He went to help her load the kids into their car seats.

"I'll follow you home and make sure everything is okay," he said after Joey was strapped into his seat.

"No, it's okay. There's no need," she insisted.

He placed his arm on the hood of her car. *Better to place it there than around her waist.* "I'll feel better making sure y'all are inside and safe for the night. It's dark."

"Fine. But there is really no need."

He was already headed to his truck. He was doing this strictly to make sure they were safe. No other reason.

Like he'd thought, she'd not realized she'd be gone until after dark and the house was blanketed in darkness as they drove up. He left his truck lights on and went to help her get the kids. Joey was, as usual, chattering up a storm.

"Let me have the keys and I'll unlock the door and turn on a porch light."

She handed it over and he had the door unlocked

and lights flipped on within moments.

"Thanks, Dalt," Joey said as he tromped inside.

"Yes, thank you. I hadn't really thought about the darkness. And it's dark out here in the country."

"You're welcome."

"Joey, let's get you ready for bed. You have to take a bath first. You're a little stinky tonight."

He glared indignantly at his mother. "I don't stink."

"Oh." She chuckled. "I beg to differ with you, little man. You smell like a little horse. And I'm sure I probably do too."

That made Joey happy. "I like horses."

"Well, I'll be going." Dalton had taken two steps back toward the front door. *This was too cozy. Too homey. Too perfect.*

If he was here much longer, he'd lose all his determination. Rae Anne had gone very still as she focused on him. And his heart pumped like an oil well that had hit the mother lode.

He took another step back.

"We had fun today."

Her voice was like silk that soothed his soul. He was in trouble; he'd said it over and over before but he knew now that he was in deeper than he'd imagined.

"Yeah, we did. Lock up behind me." He had his hand on the door when Joey walked across the room and looked up at him with his little cherub face. Dalton's heart stalled and turned over as Joey slipped his tiny hand into his.

"I show you my room."

Dalton couldn't turn away from the little boy despite that he was struggling with what he wanted and what he didn't deserve. He did not deserve to have this…not when Able Bolt no longer had the family he'd loved and adored with all his heart. Dalton had been a part of his pain; he'd been involved—involuntarily, but even that didn't bring him peace. And despite knowing it, he could not turn away from Joey, so he let the child lead him past Rae Anne and down the hallway.

Rae Anne slowly followed Joey and Dalton down the

hall. Joey had taken over the small room across the hall from the room where she slept. He had toys that Norma Sue, Esther Mae, and Adela had brought over and there was plenty of space for him to play.

Her heart gave a tug when Dalton sank to the floor and sat cross-legged with him to play with cars. Feeling a bit off-kilter, she went to put Grace to bed and then she went to run bath water for Joey. The sound of Dalton and Joey's conversation drifted to her and she smiled as she headed back to lean against the doorjamb and watch them. Dalton was so very wonderful with her little boy. He was going to make a wonderful daddy one day.

"Okay, you two. It's time for your bath now, Joey."

"But—" Joey started to complain but Dalton interrupted.

"You do like your mom asks. Cowboys always clean up after a day of riding their horse."

Immediately Joey bolted up and raced toward her as fast as his short legs could carry him. "I ready." He shed clothes as he moved past her and down the hall.

"Wow, and I mean wow!" Rae Anne watched her son strip down and head into the bathroom. "You knew the magic words."

"I try, ma'am," Dalton drawled as he tipped his hat. His lips hitched into a lopsided grin that cut straight to her heart.

Rae Anne smiled at him, and then sobered. "Please don't run off. Let me bathe him and put him in bed."

"I'll be here," he said after a hesitation. "I'll just go turn my lights out."

Rae Anne decided as she went into the bathroom to put Joey into the tub that those three words were about the most powerful words there were…other than I love you. *I'll be here.* And she knew he would be…and that made her happy.

Thirty minutes later, she found him standing beside the window, staring into the darkness. Her heart raced and her knees felt weak but she knew what she wanted as she walked to him. She had to stop herself from walking straight up to him, threading her fingers through his hair and kissing him with all of her heart.

It seemed where Dalton was concerned, her heart

followed.

"I can't tell you how much you being here for my family, for me, has meant to me." She said the words softly, and could barely hear them over the pounding of her blood rushing in her veins. She took a step closer and he watched her, his gaze locked on hers. "Today was one of the best days of my…of our lives." She took another step closer and there was a mere foot between them. She longed to touch him so badly. To caress his cheek, his jaw, feel his strong arms around her. "I—" she started and wished he'd say something. "I've never had that. Never had a man stick around and be there for me like you've done. But then, I've never known a man…" She placed her palm over his heart and found it beating as fast as her own. "A man with as big a heart as yours."

His hand came up and covered hers. "Rae…"

She wasn't sure how it happened but suddenly she found herself in his arms. He groaned, low, almost undetectable, but she was so clued in on him that she caught it as he lowered his lips to hers.

With no hesitancy, he tugged her close and made

her breathless with the power of his kiss. Emotions and feelings she'd never felt before overpowered her; as he deepened the kiss, she clung to him.

She caught herself wanting to tell him she loved him. Found herself lost in the feel and the emotion of the kiss, the way she felt cherished, safe, loved…but as her arms tightened around him, she had to remind herself that they'd only known each other for less than a month. And he'd made no overtures to her about his feelings.

Her knees went weak as he practically lifted her feet from the ground he hugged her so close and kissed her so powerfully. It was *definitely* like nothing she'd ever, ever felt before.

And never would feel in any man's arms but his.

In his arms she belonged. She'd made mistakes in her life but this was no mistake.

But, the voice in her head whispered, she had to tell him again, remind him that she didn't need to get involved… But she wanted to.

Her heart had changed since she'd last told him she didn't plan to have any more relationships. That was still true—but she now understood that it was a lifelong relationship with him that she wanted. He was good for her babies—if he hadn't been, then none of this mattered. But he was and that was the beauty of it.

And she never, ever wanted to give up what she felt here in his arms…

CHAPTER FIFTEEN

Dalton had fought his feelings but he was falling in love with Rae Anne and he wanted her. Holding her, kissing her, spending time with her gave him peace and passion, both things he'd thought he'd never have.

Her holding on to him, welcoming his kiss made him want to hang on to her for forever.

He deepened his kiss…but suddenly flashes of the wreck ambushed him and filled his mind, followed instantly by the guilt. He tore his mouth from Rae Anne but instead of turning away, he found himself saying, “I need to tell you something.”

And he knew it was right; it was time. He had to be open with her.

He forced himself to pull away and look fully at her. “I can’t deny it any longer. I have feelings for you, Rae Anne.”

“And I have feelings for you too,” she said gently.

His heart ached with the possibilities in those words. “I was involved in a wreck three years ago that I walked away from but in which a mother and son lost their lives.”

Rae Anne gasped. “Oh, Dalton, how horrible. What happened?”

He saw the compassion in her eyes and the horror, too. “It was a stormy night, much like the one that you went off the road in. The rain was coming down and the lightning was fierce. The mother was coming in the oncoming lane and as we would have passed beside each other, she lost control. It was a split second in time…their vehicle came across the center line and plowed into the side of my truck then bounced off and careened off road and hit a tree. They were both killed on impact." His hands shook as he saw it happening all over again. "I watched it happen and there had been nothing I could do to stop it."

Tears glistened in Rae Anne's eyes. "That's horrible."

He nodded, unable to say anything as memories brought on the panic attack. He'd learned to handle them, to breathe steady and to not be overwhelmed as his heart rate went frantic and the room tried to cave in around him.

"But it wasn't your fault." She reached for his hand and gripped it tightly, as if she knew how hard this was for him.

He forced words out. "Not technically, but in my mind, I replay it over and over, trying to figure out if there was anything I could have done to avoid the collision. What if I'd yanked my wheels…" He inhaled and wrapped his free hand over hers, the ones that clung tightly to his.

"That must be hard on you. I can't imagine. I'm so sorry."

"I didn't tell you this for your sympathy. I've

never told anyone about the accident. I can't bring myself to talk about it. But, you need to know, deserve to know…because I've been drawn to you from the moment I first saw you, in a deeper way than anything I've ever felt. And now I'm having to face my emotions in a way I thought I could handle."

Her eyes softened at his words. He longed to touch her cheek but he didn't.

"I believe your feelings for me are as strong as mine are for you…I know what I just felt wasn't one-sided."

"You're right." Her eyes misted and he had to harden his heart to the tenderness he saw there.

"The truth is, Rae Anne, I'm not sure I can ever feel right having a family of my own."

Her head tilted. "I don't understand. Why do you feel that way?"

"I just keep reliving the accident. There is a good man who lost his family that night. And it haunts me."

She let go of his hand and placed her palm against his cheek. "You are a good man, Dalton Borne, and I…it's too late to try to warn me. I've already fallen in love with you. And now I love you even more." He shook his head, ecstatic and torn at the same instant. She shook her head. "You can't stop what I feel any more than I can stop what I feel. And believe me, I tried not to care for you. I've made some terrible mistakes in my life and I don't feel like I deserve a man as good as you. But I can't help loving you. And now, knowing your heart and how deeply you feel things…there is no way I would want not to love you."

Dalton couldn't move. He could only take in the look in her eyes, the hope he saw there and the love. *Now what?* He wanted to pull her back into his arms and tell her he loved her too. But he didn't. He looked toward the door. "I need to go."

"Dalton?"

He cupped her face with his palms and gently kissed her lips. "I'm sorry. I need to think. I…I'll talk to you later."

And then he left. And he'd never felt more like a heel in his life.

The woman he loved had told him she loved him in the most tender way and he hadn't been able to say the words back to her.

Rae Anne didn't know exactly how to take Dalton's leaving the night after he'd told her about the accident. Her heart ached for everyone involved but from what he'd told her, there had been nothing he could have done to prevent that wreck. And yet he was suffering from what she would classify as survivor's guilt and grief. Still, he couldn't go on denying himself happiness because of the tragedy. And for him to walk out on her after she'd told him she loved him…it scared her. Scared her more than admitting to herself that she'd fallen in love with him. She had her own baggage and her own fears and yet she was facing them and praying that there was a future for her and Dalton. He had to face the truth that no amount of depriving himself of happiness would bring back that poor mother and child.

Dalton had left that night looking as though he'd just seen the ghost of Christmas Past or something. He'd been pale and his hands had been shaking as he'd grabbed for the doorknob. It had been several days—okay, it had been three days, twelve hours, and thirty minutes—since he'd walked out the door and she hadn't seen him since. Today, while the kids were napping, she was working in her small tomato patch—because she needed to work off some frustrations she was feeling. And she was extremely frustrated.

Later, she was supposed to take the kids to an event at the church that Amber had told her about during dinner the other day. The ladies in town were having an outdoor play day for all the kids in the area and especially for the kids from the shelter. Rae Anne was having trouble being motivated to do anything because she was worried about Dalton and she wasn't sure whether she was going to go.

Her mood perked up when she saw several cowboys working cattle across the pasture. She paused her hoeing and stared hopefully at the group in the distance. But Dalton wasn't among them.

As she studied them, one of the cowboys separated himself from the group and loped his black horse toward her. He sat straight in the saddle and moved easily with the horse. He was handsome, with penetrating eyes that drilled into her as he slowed the horse to a walk. He moved close to the fence and gave her an easy smile.

"Morning. I'm Treb Carson. I helped Dalton fix your car the other week. How are you doing?"

"Hello. And thank you for helping. He told me someone had helped. We're doing good and just so thankful to be here."

"Glad to hear it. I wanted to let you know we're working the cattle on the land the ranch leases on this property. We'll try not to disturb you too much."

"That's fine. Do whatever you need to do," she said, feeling more bewilderment hitting her about Dalton's not coming around.

"I should have come over earlier and let you know what we were going to be doing. Is there anything you need?"

She stared up at him. *Need*?

She *needed* Dalton.

That was the immediate thing that came to mind.

She missed him.

And she wanted him to be here. Joey asked about him every day and she didn't blame him. Dalton had become important to their lives in the short few weeks that they'd known him. Maybe she shouldn't have admitted that she loved him. But for him to suddenly just go silent and disappear…well, it hurt. And she didn't like that feeling. She'd never wanted another man to have the power to hurt her.

"No, there's nothing. But thank you for asking."

He tipped his hat. As she looked up into those amazing eyes of his that sparkled like sapphires in the glaring sunlight, she knew many a woman whose heart would be going crazy with erratic thumping over such a man. Not her; she felt nothing but an irrational irritation that he wasn't Dalton. And that wasn't Treb's fault.

"You sure you're okay?" He looked at her in concern and made her realize her emotions must be written on her face.

"Sorry, I'm fine. Just distracted today. Thanks."

Accepting her explanation, Treb turned his horse and was about to ride back to the herd when she couldn't help herself.

"Treb, wait," she called out.

He halted the horse and looked back at her over his shoulder.

"Why did you ride over here to see if I needed something?"

"Dalton asked me to check on you." He gave that easy smile again. "Wanted to make sure we weren't kicking up too much dust or anything."

"I see. Where is Dalton?"

"He's working a different section of cattle today. But he made it a point that I check on you."

She could have kicked herself for asking after him. Especially now that she knew he wasn't dead or ran off somewhere but was indeed working somewhere other than in the pasture near her.

Rae Anne hadn't been born yesterday. She knew he was sorting through their situation. But she'd told him she loved him.

Maybe she should have kept her feelings to herself.

She sighed and wished she had someone to talk to. She thought about calling Desi but she would ask too many questions and then there was always that possibility that Reese might show up and ask questions. It was just better that Desi knew nothing because from the sound of it, he'd made some really bad enemies and Rae Anne needed to separate herself from everyone he might connect her to.

Feeling alone and isolated, her mind reeling, she said good-bye to Treb and went back to her garden, attacking a clump of grass with a vengeance and chopped a tomato plant in half in the process. Staring at her poor tomato plant, she halted her hoeing and set the tool to the side so she couldn't do more damage.

"What is wrong with me?"

She was doing exactly what she'd said she'd *never* do again: focus on a man. Yes, she knew he was different than the other men who had been in her life and he'd gone through something terrible. However, her staying home worrying over what he was going to do was not helping matters and certainly not helping her.

It was time for her to get herself back on track and stop worrying about a man.

And helping with the children's festival was just the thing she needed…not attacking her poor, pathetic tomato plants.

CHAPTER SIXTEEN

The blazing sun glared down on them as Dalton stood beside the squeeze chute, holding the electric brand and waiting for Ty to let the next calf into the metal chute. They'd run a herd of calves through already and had about fifteen to go. He was ready to be finished.

Most of the time, they did their branding out on the range, like it had been done for a hundred years. But when they had a fresh load come in on a cattle trailer, it was easier to unload them into a holding pen and let them enter one by one into the squeeze chute and get their vaccinations, ear tags, and brand all in one moment. Doing it this way was monotonous and the reason Dalton preferred being out on the range.

Ty opened the gate; the calf entered the chute and he closed the gate behind it. Immediately, Rafe pulled the lever and the sides squeezed in easily around the animal to hold it safely in place. The instant it was held securely, Dalton stuck the branding iron through the rail and seared the New Horizon Ranch brand onto its hip. Rafe administered the vaccinations and put the ear tag on, and then let the calf out the front gate to join the herd.

It was quick and again, monotonous, and gave Dalton plenty of time to think—not that he'd been thinking of anything but Rae Anne since he'd walked away from her three days ago. *I love you, Dalton.* Her words clung to him… *She loved him.* Even standing here in the scalding sun with a hot iron in his hand and business to tend to, he couldn't shake the sweet sound of her voice.

Of those words.

He'd sent Treb to work the cattle around her house today when he could have been the one to lead that crew working on the range like he enjoyed the most. But he'd sent Treb instead, with instructions to check on her.

Treb. He was honorable, a great guy and single…and Dalton wanted to kick himself in the backside for sending him over there. Despite his best intentions for her, he knew he didn't want Rae Anne with any man but himself.

For the past seventy-two hours, he'd felt the weight of his past heavy on his shoulders but he'd also felt himself at a crossroads. He had to make a choice. Needed to make a choice.

"Hey Dalton," Ty called, jolting Dalton out of his thoughts. "It's your turn, buddy."

Dalton glanced at Ty and then to Rafe. Both were studying him.

"You okay?" Rafe asked.

"Yeah," Ty said. "You've been behind the ball all morning."

Dalton concentrated on his job and pressed the

branding iron to the calf's hip. The scent of searing hair filled the air as the New Horizon Ranch brand appeared on the calf…an undeniable mark.

Rae Anne's love had marked his heart. As he stared at that brand, Dalton knew he couldn't deny it. Couldn't ignore it or walk away from it.

"No, I'm not." He let the brand drop to the ground. "I have to go. I have to see Rae Anne. I have to tell her I love her."

Both Ty and Rafe grinned.

"Well, it's about time you realized it," Ty said.

"Yeah, buddy. If you could just see your face when she's around…you'd probably know what all of us have already figured out."

Dalton should have told them that he'd known it all along; it was the not deserving her that had slowed him down. But he didn't. Nope, he was already jogging toward his truck.

"We need to figure out a way to get Dalton and Rae

Anne together."

Rae Anne froze as Esther Mae's unmistakable voice drifted over the hedge where she stood.

Norma Sue grunted. "The boy has been over there on his own a bunch and then we sent him with the baby crib. It's like he's unfazed. I'm about ready to tie them in a room together till they realize they're perfect together."

"Now, girls." That was Adela. Rae Anne knew that sweet voice. "You can't rush love."

It was Esther Mae who harrumphed this time. "Who says we can't? We've done it plenty."

"But remember," Adela cautioned them again, in a hushed voice. "Rae Anne has just had a baby and none of us know what she had going on in her life that sent her running with just a few suitcases packed in her car and no other belongings."

There was a collective sigh and both Norma Sue and Esther Mae agreed.

Rae Anne couldn't move. She'd been here trying to help out. Trying to fit in and not mope but it was hard. She wanted to confide in someone. But she had her secrets and Dalton had his secrets, and she just couldn't betray what he'd told her in confidence, even if she longed for advice.

She just seemed as if she'd been struggling to find happiness all of her life and now that she could feel it so close to her and yet so far away, it was hard.

She had her children.

She had this wonderful community.

That was going to have to be enough right now. Maddie had said she and Cliff would have a baby in God's timing… Rae Anne would have to be content knowing that she would have love in God's timing.

She just wanted it to be Dalton's love.

Feeling overwhelmed, she hurried down the length of the hedge so she would come out on the far end away from where the "posse"—as they were called—wouldn't realize she'd overheard them. She now understood why they were called that. She headed away from the protection of the hedge, carrying the ball that she'd gone in search for.

"Yoo-hoo," Esther Mae called, waving wildly.

Rae Anne couldn't pretend she didn't see the enthusiastic redhead.

Reluctantly, Rae Anne walked down the hedges. "Hi y'all. Er—what are y'all up too?" she asked, despite already knowing they were plotting her love life. Which, really, she was grateful for but it scared her that too much meddling from them and Dalton might run forever.

"We're just enjoying the day." Norma Sue smiled widely.

"How are you doing?" Adela asked. "I see that sweet boy of yours is over there enjoying the bean bag toss with Maddie."

"I'm fine," she quipped. "And he loves hanging out with Maddie. She's wonderful with kids." Her voice wobbled a bit with the nerves eating a hole in her stomach.

"Oh, she sure is," Esther Mae gushed. "That Dalton is good with kids too," she added smoothly with a cute, sly smile.

He was magnificent with children, Rae Anne wanted to blurt out. “Yes he is,” she said instead, with great reserve.

“You’re lookin’ a little down.” Norma Sue studied Rae Anne far too intently. “Is there something going on we can help you with?”

“No ma’am. I’m fine.” Rae Ann’s gaze drifted longingly toward the parking lot and she wished for Dalton. Sadie called her name from where she and a group of kids were waiting on the ball. “Y’all are doing a great job with refreshments,” she said. “I better get this back.” She wasted no time jogging away from the far too perceptible scrutiny of the trio.

And it wasn’t just them. Maddie had also told her that Dalton had been very distracted at work the last couple of days. But that didn’t make her feel any better. He was staying as far away from her as he could get.

She dropped the ball; the kids raced to try to be the first to get to it. She was so lost in thought, though, that she didn’t move out of the way. Instead, she was standing in the way as ten adolescent boys plowed toward the ball—and never saw her. She was caught in the fray as they battled for the ball. Her feet got knocked out from under her and she fell backward. She yelped as she landed on her hip and pain radiated down her leg.

She might have been trampled but suddenly a deep, familiar voice said, "Whoa, hold on, boys, and let the lady up."

And just like that, the boys parted like the Red Sea and she found herself looking up at Dalton. She was stunned more by the sight of him than the fall. He knelt beside her, concern written all over his face.

"Are you alright?" Behind him, the boys were asking the same question in frantic unison as they'd just realized what they'd done.

"I'm fine. I just wasn't paying attention."

A crowd had gathered around them that included the posse, and Maddie, who was holding Joey on her hip. And Rae Anne saw Mia and Sadie behind Maddie. Amber was with the smaller kids.

Everyone was asking at once if she was okay. Joey was hollering, "Are you okay, Mama!"

It was chaos but though she was aware of everyone around her, she was focused on Dalton. *He was here.*

Not that that meant anything particularly special in terms of them…but she was just so glad to see him.

"Can you get up?" He gently took her elbow. "I'll help you."

He smelled so nice, freshly showered and a small hint of aftershave…in the middle of the day. "I thought you were working cattle today?" *Was she crazy?* The question was just there and she'd had no control in stopping it from escaping.

He was still on bended knee and she was still sitting on the hard ground, looking at him.

"I did," he said. "But then I realized I had important business to tend to that could not be put off any longer so I cleaned up and went to take care of it…but you weren't home."

"What business?" She suddenly felt as if she were

nose-diving among butterflies. Her heart started to pound.

He glanced around and then back at her. “Well, I’d hoped to do this in private. But now’s good for me. I’m sorry I panicked the other day.” He took her face into his palms; oohs and ahhs drifted about them, along with a few comments from the boys, such as “Disgusting!” and “Yuck. No kissing.”

“About what?” Esther Mae called, delight filling her voice.

A faint smile flitted across his lips as he kissed the tip of her nose and then held her gaze with his own. “I love you, Rae Anne. And I know we have some obstacles to overcome but we can handle them together,” he said very softly, for her ears only. Then, more loudly, he added, “Don’t you agree?”

She nodded. She was incapable of doing anything else in that moment.

He chuckled and brushed his lips across hers and then took her hand in his. “Rae Anne, would you do me the honor of becoming my wife? Marry me?”

Tears flooded her eyes. “I never expected to fall in love again. Only, I’ve realized since knowing you and loving you that I was never in love before and certainly never loved before. I love you, Dalton. Yes—a thousand times, yes.”

Everyone clapped and cheered. Maddie let Joey down and he raced to throw his arms around Dalton.

“Are you going to be my daddy?” he asked.

Dalton looked lovingly into his little eyes and nodded. “I sure am. Is that okay with you?”

Rae Anne thought she would melt in a puddle of tears but she held herself together.

Joey couldn’t even speak; he could only smile as big as the sun shining down on them and nod his little head before he threw his arms around Dalton’s neck and hugged him with all his might. Dalton met her gaze over Joey’s head and tears glistened in his eyes.

“I love you,” he whispered. “Let’s get Grace and go home.” He stood, still holding Joey, and helped her to her feet. Nothing hurt as they headed toward the church to get Grace from the nursery.

Everyone congratulated them and hugged them as they went.

Rae Anne felt as if she were in a dream.

Life, it turned out, had ups and downs and a mind of its own where plans were concerned. And she was very glad it did.

Excerpt from

TREB

New Horizon Ranch, Book Six

CHAPTER ONE

"Mom, stop."

"Megan Renee Tanner," her mother enunciated precisely. "I will not stop. This is the third night in a row that I've called you to find out you are spending time with the cows. Not a man. You're a young woman, but you aren't getting any younger and all your evenings shouldn't be spent with cattle. Or horses, dogs, goats, or cats for that matter. You need to be spending time with a man every once in a while or you'll become a cat lady…or—or a *cow* lady, heaven forbid."

Her mother had her on that. It was the third night on the job where she'd gotten in closer to sunrise than sunset. "I'm not having this conversation right now, Mom."

Megan transferred the phone to her other ear and held it in place with her shoulder as she lifted the tail of the high-risk show cow. It was about to give birth at any moment but so far so good. She just hoped she'd gotten the baby turned and there would be no more complications. Her arm and shoulder ached from having wrestled the calf into place and she was three days sleep-deprived. All of which she wasn't about to admit to her mother.

"You won't have the conversation about your love life because you know as well as I do that it doesn't exist. At this very moment, you're probably in the middle of pulling a calf or worse, have your arm shoved up—"

"Mom, come on. Let it go."

"I won't. You need to stop working those

ridiculous hours and get a life. A love life. You're not getting any younger and the longer you wait, the harder it'll be. Your sisters didn't wait so long…"

"Right. And look what it got them."

"That's not nice. They were happy while they were married."

"*While* being the pivotal word here. Now they're each involved in their own World War Three divorce nightmare." Both of her sisters had married men who had decided monogamy was not for them. Bad judgment seemed to run in the family…and now both sisters were devastated because of it. It had been right in front of them all along, considering their mother had gone through the trauma of divorce three times.

Three and had recently married number four. Her mom trying to sell Megan on the merits of matrimonial bliss fell way short. Megan would take the south end of a birthing cow any day to the heartache and drama that came when a marriage fell apart.

"Honey, you need to be more positive. Love is a beautiful thing."

And that was her mom. Ever the optimist when it

came to believing in happily-ever-afters. She devoured romance books and was a sap for romantic movies. Her judgment on how the world *really* worked was way off the charts.

"It doesn't last and you know it." Megan had seen the real world from the sidelines of both sisters and her mom…and she'd hardened her heart to all of it.

"When the right one comes along, it does."

"Mom, please. I need to go. This cow is about to—"

"I knew it! You *are* midwifing a heifer. Megan, you once believed in fairy tales. You loved Prince Charming."

Megan closed her eyes and counted to ten. "Mom, I was a kid. I grew up. Oops, I see a hoof—not good. I've got to go."

She hung up and groaned—both from the conversation she'd had with her mother and the fact that despite all her work on turning the calf, it was still coming out the hard way. It was going to be a rough night. But then, there was one thing her mother had never understood about Megan's career choice. She loved it. Loved everything about helping animals and being a veterinarian. She even liked the late nights…they kept her busy and that was just like she wanted it.

The sun rose in faint hues of pink and pale blue as Treb Carson rode his stallion across the open pasture toward the misty sunrise. His thoughts were troubled—he'd had another sleepless night where the dreams woke him…explosions, shouting, and the endless sound of gunfire.

It was over a year since he'd come home but he'd come to believe he'd never get the sound of war out of his mind. He'd learned there was no chance of sleep once the dreams started and he'd found riding in open country usually helped remind him that he was here, alive and blessed.

The smooth, soothing feel of the horse beneath him, the fresh air…the peaceful serenity of the morning calmed his soul…but not this morning.

He reached the peak of the hill and pulled his

horse to a halt. Resting a wrist on the saddle horn, he watched the morning come quietly over the hill. The sunrise always gave him hope…promise of a new day, a new beginning.

Today it was time to move forward, to move on with his life.

He breathed in the cool, early morning air, and continued to mull over his thoughts as the sunrise broke through the mist, gaining strength and vibrancy as it rose. He thanked God that, unlike his brother and countless others who'd given the ultimate sacrifice for their country, he'd come home alive. And now it was time to draw a line in the dirt and step across it.

Despite the lingering nightmares, it was time to make the choice to move from just existing since coming home and to start living.

His brother would want it. And as much as he wished it had been him and not Mark who had perished, that wasn't the way it was.

Treb straightened in the saddle as he made up his mind. With determination in his heart, he turned his horse around and headed back toward his home for now—the bunkhouse cabin the ranch offered its wranglers.

He decided it was time to look for a place of his own.

He enjoyed his work at the New Horizon Ranch. He liked the partners who owned the place and enjoyed this area. Mule Hollow was great cattle country and the people were amazing.

So it was time to settle down and there was no other place he'd rather do that than Mule Hollow, Texas.

His attention was suddenly caught by a large area of churned-up pasture. A sure signal that a destructive group of wild hogs had begun an attack on this area. Changing route, he followed the prints toward the woods until he saw more destroyed pastureland. They were definitely on a rip and tear path, headed toward the creek. Treb reached the water's edge and followed it until he reached the fence line that ran along the access road. The fence stopped his progress as the creek continued on under the small bridge of the road and on into the ranch's land on the other side. Prints in the mud showed that the hogs had traveled along this route.

He'd have to bring a crew out and set up cage traps to catch them and move them off the ranch.

Wild hogs bred fast and multiplied in the blink of an eye, costing ranchers massive amounts of revenue. He'd need to get on this quick. Turning back, he started toward the ranch compound when he spotted a blue truck he didn't recognize down the road under a stand of trees on the other side of the fence.

Altering his path again, he went to check it out. As he drew near, he could see a pair of cowboy boots propped up on the dash and a cowboy slumped in the seat, his head leaned back with a hat pulled down over his eyes. Probably sleeping off a night of drinking. Treb could remember a time in his early days when that might have been him. He'd come a long way since those years of rebellious living.

The truck was pulled close enough to the pipe fence that he didn't bother to dismount. Instead, he stretched over the pipe and rapped his knuckles on the half rolled-down window.

A hand came up and slowly lifted the hat a fraction. Treb stared into the wide, tired eyes of a woman. Rich amber eyes that he could imagine would shimmer in sunlight.

She yanked her booted feet to the floorboard with a bang and sat up so fast her hat fell off her head, revealing strands of caramel-colored hair that had escaped from a loose ponytail. He swallowed a lump that had formed in his throat and just stared at the beautiful, sleep-mushed female. He'd been prepared to greet a hungover cowboy, not a gorgeous woman.

"Um..." his voice faltered—*That never happened.* He tried again. "Mornin', ma'am," he drawled and tapped the front edge of his hat in greeting.

Despite her knee-jerk reaction when he'd first arrived, she was dazed too. She blinked hard and looked from him to her surroundings with sleep-dazed eyes. "Morning to you too. I guess I slept later than I thought I would."

It was clear by her words that she'd deemed him a non-threat. "I reckon." He nodded toward her and her truck. "But only if you normally lounge in bed till dawn."

"Luckily, I don't normally have to sleep in my truck." Her honey-toned eyes lit up. "Though, there was a time during vet school while in between jobs that I had to...never mind, that's a long story and you're a stranger, so I think I'll cut it off there."

She smiled and Treb felt a sharp jab of attraction. "Fair enough. But do you mind enlightening me on why you're on the New Horizon Ranch property?"

She hid a yawn and her light-brown brows crinkled as she glanced down the road and then back at him. "I just pulled onto the nearest side road. Didn't know I was trespassing. I was coming back late from trying to save a mother cow and newborn calf, and I nearly went to sleep at the wheel. I opted to pull over here to just close my eyes for a few moments. Obviously I forgot to set an alarm."

"You're a veterinarian?" The information clicked into place. He glanced at the truck, with its side panels that could house meds and equipment she might need. He hadn't paid attention to that until now.

"I am."

"And you pulled over into the trees and rolled your window down and went to sleep—that's a pretty careless thing to do. Do you realize you could have been hurt?" He couldn't believe she was an intelligent woman and had acted so carelessly.

Irritation flashed in her eyes. Then she slowly lifted her other hand—the one that she'd kept below eye level on the other side of the door until now. A Glock firearm was held securely in her grip. "I can take care of myself."

If he wanted to, he could have that stupid gun away from her before she could blink her pretty eyes, but he didn't point that out. "So, I assume you know how to use that?"

"I do." Her eyes narrowed. "And I'm not in the least bit afraid to use it. My war vet granddaddy believed in making all his granddaughters expert marksman. Believe me, no one is going to mess with me."

"I'll point out that you were sleeping harder than a bear in hibernation when I rapped on your half-opened window. I could have had an arm through that open glass before you had one eye open."

She cocked her head and studied him. "And I'd have shot you."

"More likely you'd have shot off your toe or something when I startled you."

"Maybe. But *then* I'd have shot you." She stared at him in challenge.

His brows dipped and he was at a loss for words that she would put herself into such a vulnerable situation. He'd seen far too much in his combat tour to make any kind of sense of someone just acting downright senseless.

"All I can say is I hope this isn't common practice for you and I'd appreciate it if you'd put that thing away for now. I'm not here to hurt you. I work on the ranch."

She held his gaze for a long moment then slowly lowered the gun. "Sorry, but a girl can't be too careful."

"Careful? Honey, you were careless."

Fire flashed again. "I guess you can have your own opinion. Look, I need a cup of coffee." She cocked her head out the window, staring hard at his horse. "You wouldn't happen to have a hot cup of coffee in there, would you?"

He realized she'd zeroed in on the thermos that stuck out of his saddlebag. She opened her truck door and got out and he found himself at a loss for words again as his gaze drifted down her long legs and shapely figure. She wore a simple T-shirt and jeans that hugged her curves. The jeans were tucked into well-worn boots. She looked every inch the cowgirl vet that she was. And as spunky as she'd appeared so far.

She grabbed the top rail of the pipe fence that separated them, then lifted her face to him. He just stared down at her, taking in her small splattering of freckles and clear skin.

"Is there anything in it?" she asked again, prompting him when he hadn't answered her.

He yanked his thoughts off her attributes. "I do, as a matter of fact."

"Would you consider sharing it with me? I need to get back home and shower before I start my daily rounds and coffee right now would be heaven sent. I'm truly grateful that you showed up and woke me or I would have been late for work."

Treb found himself grinning at the anticipatory way she was eyeing his thermos of coffee. Obviously coffee had the power to erase any displeasure she'd had with him.

"Glad I could help," he drawled and tried not to get lost in those eyes. Instead, he tugged the thermos from his saddlebag and unscrewed the attached cup.

"Hold on," she snapped. She spun back to her truck, leaned inside and a moment later, she whirled back to him, holding a paper cup up triumphantly. "Bingo! Coffee to go."

She popped the lid off and poured out the few drops of leftover coffee. "My lone cup from last night—it's been far too long ago." She held it up to him and smiled.

Treb stared down at her. That engaging smile, those now sparkling eyes…he could only imagine how they'd sparkle when she wasn't worn out.

"A-hem." She cleared her throat dramatically and wiggled the cup, drawing his attention to the fact that he'd been staring and not pouring.

Too quickly, he reached for the cup and his fingers wrapped completely around hers. A kick-in-the-stomach-from-a-bucking-bull slam of electrical attraction raced up his arm, jarring him with its impact. What was up with him? He hadn't reacted like this to a woman in…well, in ever.

Her eyes widened and flashed with instant energy, making him almost positive she'd felt it too. She slipped her fingers out of his and focused on the coffee. "It smells fabulous."

He poured the coffee. "Here you go. That should clear your mind." He placed it into her hands. Steam curled from the cup and she was very careful taking it from him. He didn't miss that she was also very careful to avoid contact with him again.

Just as he was careful not to touch her either.

"Heavenly." She breathed in the scent of the coffee and then pursed her lips and took a sip.

His gut tightened as he watched her and was startled when hot coffee spilled on his thigh. "Hot," he bit out and yanked his gaze from watching her to concentrate on pouring himself a cup.

"Careful," she warned. "This is amazingly hot. That's a great thermos. You'll have to tell me what brand so I can get myself one. It could come in handy on lone, late-night calls." She took another sip. "Thanks so much. I've got to go. My dog, Archie, is probably wondering what happened to me."

She took another long sip, smiled charmingly at him.

He just stared down at her, frozen in place as she turned and climbed back into her truck...*Archie was one lucky dog.*

"Drive safe," he called.

She lifted the cup in salute. "Duty calls." She cranked her truck and shifted it into gear.

Treb sipped his coffee, trying to appear unaffected, as he watched her make a wide U-turn and head back down the access road, disappearing in a cloud of dust.

He almost thought he'd dreamed her. That the escapade actually hadn't happened.

But he knew even in his crazy dreams that he'd never have dreamed up this woman. He realized then that he didn't even know her name. And she didn't know his.

But he would.

She had been interesting, though a little soft in the head if she believed she was safe out here. There were crazies in this world, even in small towns. Common sense was something that everyone needed to use and gun-toting-vet-lady hadn't shown she had any to use.

New Horizon Ranch did a lot of business with the vet clinic. He hoped they didn't have any of their champion stock that needed looking after while Susan Turner was on maternity leave. He'd have to mention this to the owners of the ranch. And after that, it wasn't any of his concern. Not until he had his own herd. Then he'd have reasons to be concerned about whether he wanted her working on his animals. Until then, it was someone else's call.

He poured out his coffee and twisted the lid onto the thermos, still very aware of the way he'd reacted to her touch. And very aware that he wouldn't be acting on that attraction.

A woman who worked all hours of the day and

night and sometimes slept in her truck was not the type of woman he had an interest in—even if he was attracted to her.

He was almost back to the ranch compound before it dawned on him that he hadn't thought about his past or bad dream since she'd pulled her hat off her head and turned those eyes of hers on him.

More Books by Debra Clopton

Turner Creek Ranch Series
Treasure Me, Cowboy (Book 1)
Rescue Me, Cowboy (Book 2)
Complete Me, Cowboy (Book 3)
Sweet Talk Me, Cowboy (Book 4)

New Horizon Ranch Series
Her Texas Cowboy (Book 1)
Rafe (Book 2)
Chase (Book 3)
Ty (Book 4)
Dalton (Book 5)
Treb (Book 6)
Maddie's Secret Baby (Book 7)
Austin (Book 8)

Cowboys of Ransom Creek
Her Cowboy Hero (Book 1)
Bride for Hire (Book 2)
Cooper (Book 3)
Shane (Book 4)
Vance (Book 5)
Drake (Book 6)
Brice (Book 7)

Texas Matchmaker Series

Dream With Me, Cowboy (Book 1)

Be My Love, Cowboy (Book 2)

This Heart's Yours, Cowboy (Book 3)

Hold Me, Cowboy (Book 4)

Be Mine, Cowboy (Book 5)

Marry Me, Cowboy (Book 6)

Cherish Me, Cowboy (Book 7)

Surprise Me, Cowboy (Book 8)

Serenade Me, Cowboy (Book 9)

Return To Me, Cowboy (Book 10)

Love Me, Cowboy (Book 11)

Ride With Me, Cowboy (Book 12)

Dance With Me, Cowboy (Book 13)

Windswept Bay Series

From This Moment On (Book 1)

Somewhere With You (Book 2)

With This Kiss (Book 3)

Forever and For Always (Book 4)

Holding Out For Love (Book 5)

With This Ring (Book 6)

With This Promise (Book 7)

With This Pledge (Book 8)

With This Wish (Book 9)

With This Forever (Book 10)

With This Vow (Book 11)

About the Author

Bestselling author Debra Clopton has sold over 2.5 million books. Her book OPERATION: MARRIED BY CHRISTMAS has been optioned for an ABC Family Movie. Debra is known for her contemporary, western romances, Texas cowboys and feisty heroines. Sweet romance and humor are always intertwined to make readers smile. A sixth generation Texan she lives with her husband on a ranch deep in the heart of Texas. She loves being contacted by readers.

Visit Debra's website at www.debraclopton.com

Sign up for Debra's newsletter at
www.debraclopton.com/contest/

Check out her Facebook at
www.facebook.com/debra.clopton.5

Follow her on Twitter at @debraclopton

Contact her at debraclopton@ymail.com

If you enjoyed reading *Dalton*, I would appreciate it if you would help others enjoy this book, too.

Recommend it. Please help other readers find this book by recommending it to friends, reader's groups and discussion boards.

Review it. Please tell other readers why you liked this book by reviewing it on the retail site you purchased it from or Goodreads. If you do write a review, please send an email to debraclopton@ymail.com so I can thank you with a personal email. Or visit me at: www.debraclopton.com.

Made in the USA
Monee, IL
29 September 2020